Where the Broken Lie

Derek Rempfer

IMMORTAL INK
PUBLISHING

An Immortal Ink Publishing, LLC Book
13302 Winding Oak Court, Suite A
Tampa, FL 33612
http://www.immortalinkpublishing.com

DEDICATION

To all of you I love.
For all of you I miss.

Today

I see half the beauty I used to see and twice as much despair.
I've got twice as much ambivalence and half as much of care.
I hear half your words of sympathy, but none of them console.
I've got half a heart and half a mind and half of me is hole.

This cross is twice as heavy, but I'm feeling half as strong.
Today is half of yesterday, but the nights are twice as long.
I'm stumbling through the darkness only half way in control.
I've got half a heart and half a mind and half of me is hole.

I burn with twice the rage and I'm only half forgiving.
I've got twice as many children, only half of them are living.
I have twice the faith I used to have but pray with half a soul,
Cause it's hard to feel complete when only half of you is whole.

Lost

Sometimes lost is just a word. Other times it's life changing. It's the sharp edge of forever.

"KA-TIE! KA-TIE! KA-TIE COOO-PERRR!"

"What about the park—has anybody checked at the park?"

"Yes, they checked the park. She's not there."

"What about Ike's? Anybody look up there?"

"Ike's closed two hours ago."

"Well maybe she got locked inside somehow. Somebody should go check."

At some point, I fell asleep on the living room couch, which was where I was when Mom nudged me awake in the early darkness of the next morning. She didn't speak. She didn't have to. A mother can tell her child a lot of things with just a look.

And my mother's look told me that Katie Cooper was dead.

***

There were things inside me once that are gone forever now, replaced by something harder. It started that day. Katie Cooper's death was the day I started to die, and Ethan's death is what finished me off.

I walk into the room where my only son lies in an open casket. It is the second hardest thing I will ever have to do.

Tammy couldn't bring herself to see him like this, so I come here on my own, which I actually prefer. I can be selfish with my pain. Wrap myself up in it without having to be strong for anyone else. It will be our final moment as father and son.

I have never hyperventilated before, but this must be what it feels like. My chest heaves, my stomach swells, and I can't catch my breath. Swallowed screams cut my throat.

I edge toward him.

Ethan's face is as bruised and battered as it had been at the hospital two nights earlier. He will never heal. There is nothing for me to do but say goodbye. I stand over him and cry. My tears fall onto his face and I rub them into his skin so that a part of me is buried within him.

I kiss him one last time and stroke his hair. I tell him I love him. And then I turn and walk out of that room where my only son lies in an open casket. It's the hardest thing I will ever have to do.

I will never heal—old Tucker is every bit as dead as his son.

Who the hell am I now?

The answer to that question, perhaps, can be found in Willow Grove.

***

There's an old couple that lives in an old house in a little town in the Midwest. The old couple are my grandparents and the house is my childhood home, which Grandpa and Grandma bought back into the Gaines family when my mom remarried. The town—Willow Grove, Illinois—is where I attended my first day of kindergarten, my last day of high school, and all school days in between. I have walked its sidewalks as a son and as a father. On its streets, I have pulled my Radio Flyer and driven my Dodge Caravan. In its open fields, I have lain. The town remembers me and, like a lonely old man, it reminds me of my forgotten stories whenever I visit. I have gone back to this place more times than I have left it, and it will probably always be this way, for my childhood still lives and breathes in the green grasses and the tall trees of this—my hometown.

It's the first Saturday of May, and the mid-spring air warms my skin. The citizens of Willow Grove are planting flowers, painting shutters, riding bikes. As I drive through town, I recognize faces, but I don't wave. Try to not even look, but can't help myself. The Abbot's house, once pea green, is now sweet-corn yellow. The Huber's driveway is freshly blacktopped. A few other changes here and there, but mainly everything is the same as ever.

Old Man Keller rolls down the middle of Fourth Street on his Cub

Cadet as if he owns the road, and I suppose an argument can be made that he does. That old lawn tractor has probably logged more hours on these streets than any other vehicle in town history. He has been mowing lawns in this town since he was a kid, back when lawn mowing was a much quieter whirring and snippy activity, and when the Old Man doesn't have a lawn to mow, he rides around town on that old tractor.

He stops his Cub Cadet in its tracks and waves for me to slow down.

"How you doin', Tuck?" he yells over a sputtering engine.

"All right, I guess. How about you, Alvin?"

"Good, good, doin' good. Well, I heard you might be coming back for a stay. It'll be nice seeing you around."

I've spent too many years in Willow Grove to be surprised by Old Man Keller knowing about my visit.

"Yep. See you around," I say, pulling away.

Nice enough old guy, Keller, but I sure can't imagine living his grass-mowing life. His wife is a nurse at the county hospital so cutting grass in the summer and plowing snow in the winter probably paid enough for the Old Man and the Old Woman. I often wonder what kind of thoughts the Old Man has riding atop that tractor. Plenty of time for thinking, that's for sure. At some point, you've got to figure he asked the good Lord what his life's purpose was and the answer he got back was *Cut the grass, Alvin.*

Rather than cross the railroad tracks that divide the town, I slow to a stop when I reach them and take long looks each way, wondering where those trains ever come from and where they ever go. The trains never stop in Willow Grove, they just roar through. It was along these tracks that Katie Cooper's body had been found so many years ago.

As my eyes linger on the empty landscape of rock and weed, gruesome images of blood and flesh play in my mind, fabricated long ago to fit with the stories I had heard. Katie's half-naked body lying in the tall grass, a cluster of interested crows cawing from the telephone wires above. Her eyes open wide in a dead stare and her mouth agape, framed by blood-crusted lips. Those green eyes had looked into mine countless times. Those pretty lips had kissed my cheek just once.

Off in the distance, a single light flickers like a solitary star. Perhaps it's Katie or Ethan. Who knows? The light grows larger, moves toward me. Loud bells ding-ding-ding, and the crossing gates lower. I let my foot off the brake and roll off the tracks, just under one of the gate's falling arms.

***

I slow my car to a stop on the blacktop driveway that had just been a mess of grass and gravel when I had lived here. And even from here I can see that the stairs leading up to the second-story sun porch thirst for paint and would easily soak up two or three coats.

It's such a warm secret of a room, that sun porch. Grandma once told me that this house had served as the home and office of the town doctor many years ago. The story goes that the doctor had a daughter who had contracted tuberculosis and was unable to leave her bed, much less the house. The doctor had the sun porch built so his little girl could spend her waking (and dying) hours nearer to the outdoors she so loved and missed. I didn't hear that story until many years after I'd moved out of the house, and I'm glad because it would have made the room something other than it was for me.

The little girl supposedly died in that room, but you couldn't feel it. You didn't feel the hopelessness of the little girl who died in that room. You felt the love of the father who built it. Surely it was a desperate and helpless love at the time, but not anymore. Now it's simply love in its purest form. Still, I can see the mourning father defiantly pouring his heart, his soul, and all things earthly into providing his dying child a warm room closer to the heavens but still within his reach. Like some sort of desperate compromise offered to God with knee bent and fist raised.

May this room stand forever.

Such a beautiful place, this home. I'm beginning to feel connected to something for the first time in weeks.

***

Inside, Grandma and Grandpa are sitting in the living room, doing what they do: her knitting in her chair and him reading a magazine with a hooked fish on the cover. The television isn't on, but the local news blares from the kitchen radio. Savory smells float in from the kitchen.

Grandma puts her knitting to the side and greets me with a hug. "I was beginning to wonder if you was lost."

"Hi, Grandma." I bend to kiss her. "No, not lost, just taking a look around, you know. Those back stairs could use some paint."

"Yep, it's on your list," she says.

"List?"

Grandpa rises with one strong hand extended, the other clasped on my shoulder. "Oh, she's got a whole list of things for you to do." He tips back in an exaggerated manner and looks up at me as if he's staring at a California Redwood. "My goodness, I don't think I'll ever get used to having to look up at you, Tuck. At least I'm still better looking."

"No arguments there," I say, enduring Grandpa's overly firm handshake. "So what's this list about, Grandma?"

"Your list of chores," she says. "You didn't think you was going to board here for free, did you, Tuck?"

She laughs, and it's *her* laugh. High pitched and bursting, as if she's gotten a love pinch on the behind. That's how Grandma Gaines always laughs. As if something inside her can't be contained.

"No, I suppose not, Grandma. So I'm painting the back stairs, what else do you have planned for me?"

"One thing at a time, dear. One thing at a time."

***

... so Tucker is back in Willow Grove. Not for the first time, of course, but it had been a while. And it always made him nervous. Even now. Seeing Tucker meant being reminded of Katie Cooper and everything that happened back then. That overplayed nightmare memory still so fresh in his

mind and in the collective mind of Willow Grove …

***

The next morning, with Grandma knitting and Grandpa tinkering with something in the garage, I go off on my own. I'm worn out from chasing my racing thoughts, so I try to walk away from them instead.

I don't get far.

I stop in the middle of Madison Street and quietly watch as a man I once knew weeds his flower garden. On hands and knees, clawing and scratching at earth with a harnessed vigor, he tosses the flower killers over his shoulder with something like ruthlessness. At least that's how I see it. To most, an old man tending his garden represents peaceful nurturing. But when I see Howard Cooper, I remember his beautiful daughter lying inside an open casket with her hands folded unnaturally across her chest, which I really did see. And I see her violent death, which I did not see but imagined a thousand times.

He stands, and he's not as tall as he once was. He takes off his cap and reveals what few hairs the years had left him with. From a side pocket of his overalls, he pulls out a red handkerchief and uses it to wipe his brow and his near-bald head. He turns in my direction and squints at me as hard as one might squint at the sun. I want to call out to him but can't decide whether I should refer to him as Mr. Cooper or Howard. It would be silly for me to call him Mr. Cooper, so I quickly rehearse saying, "Howard" under my breath. I should call him Howard. I'm a grown man, after all.

"Hi, Mr. Cooper," I say.

"Well, I'll be," he says with a smile that crept in from a memory. He tosses his gloves on the ground and waves me over.

"It's good to see you, Mr. Cooper."

"It's good to be seen."

He keeps his eyes on me but sends his voice inside the house. "Mother, come on out here in the garden. I want to show you how things have grown."

I smile and look down where I see a feather laying at my feet. No, not *at* my feet. *On* my feet. My breath catches in my throat and I feel my smile fade.

Mr. Cooper puts his hand on my back and walks me toward his house. But not before I bend down and pick up that feather.

***

A month after losing Ethan, Tammy and I were desperate to find some sort of meaning in his death. The universe owed us something it didn't seem willing to pay. And as the universe consistently fell short of our expectations, we consistently lowered them.

In our never-ending quest for signs and wonders, Tammy and I had visited Lady Denise, a local psychic. She lived out in the country in a two-story farmhouse shingled in an uninspired brown. The roof was checkered with missing tiles and had a slight left-to-right downward slant. The house was surrounded by several small shacks and a large hay barn that at one time must have been proud with red but now stood gray and humbled. The gravel driveway curved around to the back of the house where we saw any variety of animals wandering the yard. Cats, chickens, a pig, wild turkeys, goats, geese, and even llamas. On the far side of the lot was a kennel that housed two chesty Rottweilers who seemed ready to dispel us of any "bark worse than bite" notions we might have had.

We got out of the car and walked toward the house where the front door swung loose from its top hinge. Invisible chimes jingled, and the gentle wind softly proclaimed. The dogs stopped barking and Lady Denise suddenly appeared before us in the doorway with a black lab at her side.

"Oh, hi. I'm Tucker Gaines, and this is my wife, Tammy. I called yesterday."

She was barefoot and dressed in blue jeans and a white t-shirt. She had long white-blonde hair, bright red fingernails and toenails, and contradicted the image of a psychic I had in my head.

"Have a seat at the table," she said with a welcoming gesture. "I'm going to get something to drink. Can I get you anything?"

"No, thank you," Tammy and I both said.

We moved to the dining room where a tabby cat slinked over and curled itself around my leg. The house was cluttered and gave me an uneasy feeling that kept me from sitting down or touching anything. The rooms felt old, and rays of sunlight exposed the dust that hung in the air. On one light-blue dining room wall hung a painting of a close-eyed Virgin Mary holding a baby and resting on a cloud surrounded by an army of angels.

The front door slammed shut behind us. We spun around to see that Lady Denise had somehow crept back into the room without our noticing and was already sitting on the opposite side of the dining room table, a half-empty glass of lemonade in front of her.

"You are being followed," she informed us without smile or sinister. "Please, have a seat."

Suddenly, I felt silly and sinful. What was I really expecting to happen here? I glanced around for a crystal ball.

There was nothing dramatic in our forty-five minutes with Lady Denise, but it did bring us peace somehow. She had a quiet, soothing manner and commanded trust when she spoke. Probably because the things she spoke were things we wanted to hear. As we were leaving, Lady Denise put her hand on my left wrist and, eyes bright with conviction, told me to watch for feathers.

"Feathers will be Ethan's way of letting you know he is with you."

"Thank you for this," I said awkwardly. "How much do we owe you?"

"Nothing. I don't charge for grief counseling. It's my way of giving thanks for my gifts."

One evening a week later, I sat alone in my basement dizzy on vodka. Any sense of peace and acceptance that Lady Denise had managed to instill in me was long gone. Her words and comfort diluted with drink until they lost all potency. A sudden fury welled up from inside me and

I began punching the pillow I had been clutching. When my rage burned out, I tossed the pillow to the floor and sat back against the couch. Then, right in front of my face, one perfect tiny white pillow-feather drifted down and landed in my open palm as soft and as light as an answered prayer.

***

Mrs. Cooper pours me lemonade from a glass pitcher. Her dark auburn hair has thin streaks of gray, which run exactly where you would paint them were you the painter. She puts the pitcher down on a small wrought iron table and tucks some of that lovely hair behind her ears the same way her daughter used to. The same way my daughter does now. The same way every little girl ever has. The corners of Betty Cooper's mouth used to curl upward in a beautiful Mona Lisa sort of way, and I used to wonder what secrets must be hidden away in there. I say that they used to curl upward because I notice while eating her cookies and drinking her lemonade that they don't anymore. There's a stormy torment that clouds her face these days. She's every bit the small town beauty she had been years back, but behind her glassy green eyes there is a sadness that had not always been there. A gentle anguish where there had once been a flowing peace.

"We heard about your loss, Tucker," she says, sitting with Mr. Cooper and me at the table on the back porch. "And we're so sorry."

"Thank you, Mrs. Cooper."

"You were always such a good boy," she says with a shake of her head and a frown that says "shame on the world."

"You're good people, too, Mrs. Cooper," I say. "And so was Katie."

Then we talk about Katie, and I tell them the story of the first time I met their little girl.

***

I was never one of those boys who thought girls were icky—not for even one day of my life. For me, little girls were always the melt away sweetness of a cotton candy at the county fair. They were red balloons and white doves and every other thing that rose high and lifted our eyes with them. They were bows and ribbons and every other thing that colored and adorned. And a pretty little girl has always turned me into a dopey little boy.

The story of the prettiest little girl of all begins in the summer of 1981, the year that I fell in love with Katie Cooper. The moving van was parked in the driveway of the Duffy's old place across the street, and I rode by on my bike a few times to see if I could catch a glimpse of our new neighbors. On my third trip around, I saw a kid my age struggling to carry cardboard boxes piled high above his head.

"Hey, you need some help with that?" I yelled, steering out of the street and into the yard.

I jumped off my bike and let it coast-crash to a stop as I ran over to catch the top box that was sliding off. I caught it just before it hit the ground and cradled it under my arm like a fumbled football.

"Good catch, huh?" I asked, lifting myself up to see my newest Wiffle ball victim. I had been expecting to find a boy behind that stack of boxes, of course. What I found instead was the prettiest little girl of all, and I thought so the second I saw her freckle-faced smile peek out from behind the boxes that concealed her.

"Not bad," she said. "Of course, it is the lightest box."

I swallowed hard and a thousand spiny creatures crawled up and down my back, my neck, my limbs. With an open mouth, I gulped out a loud and stupid laugh. "HUH-HUH-HUH!"

She gave me a queer look and then a smirk that made me feel as though she had considered me, sized me up, and decided to like me all in an instant.

"I can carry a heavier box," I said. Then added, "I mean, if you want."

And thus began my first great romance.

***

"Yep," I say, "I spent about one-tenth of a second disappointed that Katie wasn't a boy and then I was head over heels in love with her every second after."

Tears well in Betty Cooper's eyes, and she puts a hand to her mouth.

"Oh, I'm sorry, Mrs. Cooper."

She gives me a mock frown and points her scolding finger at me. "Don't you dare apologize for telling me you loved my little girl. You were the only boy who ever got to."

Mr. Cooper gently rubs his wife's back and, for the second time in my life, I feel like my love for Katie Cooper is a gift I have given. And, like that first time, I got a kiss on the cheek in return.

"Now," Mrs. Cooper says with a sniff and a wipe of her nose. "Who wants some chocolate chip cookies?"

I spend the next hour drinking lemonade and eating chocolate chip cookies with Howard and Betty Cooper. I tell them everything I remember about their daughter, and they listen to me like wide-eyed little children hearing something brand new in a favorite story they have heard a hundred times before. So many stories that I had somehow forgotten to remember. We find joy inside those memories. Laughter, too. And as I walk back to my grandparents later that afternoon, I find myself wondering where Tammy and I will find our Ethan joy and laughter. Years from now, what stories will we comfort each other with? What stories *can* we comfort each other with, when we have none?

But there would be a story. One that we never could have imagined. And one that offered nothing in the way of comfort.

The Father Below

I'm sitting on a bench at the playground near my old elementary school when a child's voice calls out, "Hey, Mister!"

The voice isn't coming from memory—where I often live these days—but rather from one of the nearby swings. I had been alone here just moments ago, but somehow this little girl has snuck in under my radar.

"Yes?"

"Whatcha doin'?" she asks between smacks of bubble gum. I guess her to be about ten years old.

"I'm–sorry—what?"

The little girl pumps her legs and soars higher into the Willow Grove sky, speaking only when she reaches the highest point of her swing. "WHAT ARE … YOU DOING … HERE?"

Then she stops and sticks both legs straight out in front of her as if gliding in for a landing.

"Oh, uh, I don't know. Just thinking, I guess."

"Thinking?" she asks.

She pumps hard one more time and launches herself from the swing high into the air. Higher than I would have thought possible, and my heart skips a beat for her safety. A spastic gasp escapes me, and both arms reach out involuntarily as if to catch her from afar. Such a rise and fall would surely result in sprains or breaks for me, but she is without the rigidness and doubt of adulthood; she lands softly and safely, almost fluttering to the ground. Then, in a glorious 'stuck the landing' sort of way, she raises her arms high and lifts a smiling face to the heavens.

Bravo. I clap for her achievement.

"Thinking, huh? That's what you came here to do?" she asks.

Walking toward me now, I see that she's taller than I originally thought. And her hair—which had looked sandy brown in the sun-light—grows darker as she approaches. She gives me a reproachful stare that makes it clear I have disappointed her. As if she had been looking for me to be evidence that all adults weren't hopeless bores.

"Well," she says, "what are you thinking about?"

A good question without a good answer. I had come here to think about everything and nothing at all.

"I'm not sure."

"That seems dumb."

I laugh and concede, "Yeah, I suppose it does."

"I came here to swing." Then, after a moment, she adds, "I don't think you came here to think. I think you came here to sit."

"You know what? You're right," I say, rising from the bench. "No more sitting. It was nice talking to you."

As I walk away, she calls out to me one more time.

"Hey, mister?"

"Yes?"

She blows a bubble and pops it with her pinky finger. "I'm just saying that if a person comes to the playground, maybe they should swing or something. That's all."

***

... seeing Tucker with the girl on the swing. It was like going back in time. Though this girl didn't bare any real resemblance to Katie Cooper. Yet there was something about her. Maybe it was her innocence. Her naiveté. It was reminiscent of Katie and it both excited and sickened him. All at once it was that summer again. And that secret was fresh and new. The sleeping monster inside of him stirred. Alive and kicking like a newborn baby ...

***

After dinner, I head to my bedroom. I love my grandparents, but cannot tolerate anyone's company right now. Even theirs.

When I talked to Grandma on the phone about staying here for a lit-tle while, she didn't ask for how long, she didn't ask why, she didn't ask anything. She just told me that they'd be glad to have me and that she'd make up my old room. So that's where I slept that first night—in the same room I slept in as a boy. I could have asked for the larger bedroom that had belonged to my little sister Heather when we were kids, but there was less comfort in that thought.

Being there again is a strange sensation. I almost convince myself that I'm a little boy again and that my brother and sister are in their rooms down the hall, not yet asleep. A feeling of being safe settles on me, like when I used to crawl into bed with my Mom and Dad during a thunderstorm. Nestled between them. Softness on one side, strength and shelter on the other. Like being inside of God.

As I drift off, I try to feel like that little boy. Try to think his thoughts, sleep his sleep, dream his dreams. But I can't. That little boy is dead.

Like every day of my new life, I have been thinking of Ethan. But it's always in the company of others, and I need to be alone. I also need to be drunk.

Like every day of my new life, I cry. I imagine for the ten-thousandth time how lonely and frightened he must have been. How alone and forsaken he must have felt in those final moments before giving himself up to death.

Like every day of my new life, I pray. They are bitter and angry words spit out through tears and snot and gasping breaths. I try to stick with the Lord's Prayer, but vodka makes me angry and angry is my natural state these days, so I am angry on angry. I condemn God and then pray for his forgiveness. I curse Him and then I thank Him for all my blessings. Most of all, though, I question Him. You could convince me that Ethan dying is not God punishing, but you could not convince me that it wasn't His allowing. And, truth be told, I hate Him for it.

For the second night of my new life, I sleep alone. Sleep, that is, until I awake gasping for air. My choking dream has returned. Head throbbing, chest heaving, I spring upright in bed and suck in as much air as my lungs can hold. The breath-taking nightmare is much more intense.

The muscles in my throat are tight and achy. They hurt so much that my neck is sensitive to the touch.

I flip on the nightstand light, pull the covers back off my legs, and look at my angel-son, skin-painted on the inside of my left leg above the ankle. I fold my leg toward me and gently rub a thumb across his cherub face. Breathing easier now, I speak his name out loud just to hear myself say it. So that my ears might know the sound of the name. So that my tongue might know the feel of the name. So that this world might not forget the name.

"Ethan," I repeat.

The feather from the Cooper's yard trembles on the nightstand. I pick it up, close my hand around it tightly, and turn out the light.

> *Dancing butterfly*
> *Delicate and free*
> *Carry this prayer to*
> *The highest tree*
> *A prayer of love*
> *That my son might know*
> *His Father above and*
> *His father below*
>
> *Blackbird's brother*
> *Heart on wing*
> *Carry this prayer to*
> *The King of Kings*
> *Lift to the clouds these*
> *Words of love*
> *From the father below to*
> *The Son above*
>
> *Lord of Lords and*

King of Kings
Accept this prayer of
Cloud and wings
And send a sign so that
I might know
That the son above loves
The father below.

The next morning, my first thought upon waking is that this bed had been a lot more comfortable when I was ten. My second thought is that I had not called home the night before.

Tory answers on the first ring, and we talk for a couple minutes about a hundred different things.

"Daddy, guess what?"

"What?"

"Hillary got a new dog."

"Oh, did she? I thought she already had a dog."

"She did have a dog. Now she has two dogs. We don't have any dogs because dogs wipe their butts on the carpet and not toilet paper and you don't like that, Daddy. And, Daddy, guess what?"

"What?"

"Smoking is bad for you. I'm glad you're living a tobacco-free life, Daddy."

"You're right, Sweetie, smoking is bad for you."

"And, Daddy, guess what?"

"Sweetie, can I talk to Mommy?"

"Okay. Love you, Daddy. Bye."

"Love you, too, Sweetie."

She hands the phone to her mother.

"Hello." Neither warm nor cool.

"Hi, Tam."

"Hi."

"How are you doing?" I ask. "Miss me yet?"

"I was missing you before you left."

"I can believe that. But I think maybe you were looking forward to missing me a little more."

"Maybe a little," she says, and I hear the smile that her words passed through.

"Are you doing okay?"

"We're doing fine. Tory's been asking lots of questions about both you and Ethan."

"What do you tell her?"

"I tell her that we'll see you soon and Ethan someday."

She asks how I am and what I had been doing, if I was still drinking. My answers were short like she knew they would be. Some truth, some lies. "You're still planning on coming over for Mother's Day, right?" I ask.

"Yeah, sure."

"Good. I can't wait to see you guys. I'll call you again tomorrow, okay?"

I wait for Tammy to hang up first and then sit there and listen to the dial tone. *That should be the official sound of "Death,"* I think to myself. But there had been life on the other end of that phone just a minute ago. *"And Tory should be the official sound of "Life."* Even when mundane, there is so much power in life. Sometimes *especially* when mundane. The normal thoughts of a four year-old could be so life affirming. That little girl makes me happy.

***

"So? How are you doing?" Grandma asks.

We're in the car, returning from Glidden where we had been grocery shopping. She wants me to bring up Ethan. I'm not going to.

"Fine," I say. "Thanks again for letting me stay with you guys for a few nights."

"Oh, that's no problem. It's nice having some company. Your grandfather and I don't get many visitors anymore, you know."

At forty miles-per-hour, the six-mile trip from Glidden to Willow Grove can be excruciating, which is exactly what the drivers in the line of cars behind Grandma are thinking, I'm sure. That stretch of route 38 has just enough curves and hills to make passing a near impossibility. When we come upon the one straight and flat stretch of that part highway, three cars whiz past, each with horns a-honking.

"Oh, those must be friends of yours," Grandma says. "They were waving."

"Yeah, and they think I'm number one, too," I mumble.

As we approach my old high school, Grandma slows even more and points at the small farmhouse across the road from it.

"You see that there? Ain't that something?"

She's pointing at a great big red hay barn that has been around as long as I can remember. Except now it has a hole right through its center.

"Wow, what the heck happened there?"

"Them tornadoes we had a few weeks back. Two touched down. One got the best of that barn."

What a strange sight to behold. Like a freight train had driven right through it.

"It looks like God tipped that tornado on its side and drilled a hole through its center," I say.

"I believe God does things like that sometimes."

"I believe God can be random and cruel, if that's what you mean."

"There's always a purpose, Tucker," she says with the kind of look that only the elderly can offer. Her eyes are as blue with promise as they must have been the day she was born. Those eyes have not aged at all, but the lids above them are heavy with years and the skin below them sags.

"Really? And what's the purpose of putting a hole through the middle of that barn, Grandma?"

"Maybe to show us that it survived," Grandma says. "That barn will come down some day, but it won't be because of that tornado or the hole that it left. It still stands, even with the hole right through its center. And besides, now you can see what's on the other side of it. You never could before."

"I looked, Grandma. I didn't see anything on the other side."

"I know, Tucker. That's what bothers me. People who don't see nothing on the other side of something like that, well, that's about what they live for—nothin'."

When we get back, I send Grandma inside and carry the groceries in myself. Howard Cooper, in his garden once again, smiles and waves at me. Seems like he spends all his time these days tending to those plants and flowers. No radio playing. No headphones. Just Howard Cooper and the tools he needs to help things grow. I didn't remember him being such an avid gardener. As a kid, I suppose I wouldn't have noticed one way or the other. He could have been a gardener all along. Or he could have started after Katie died.

I feel an overwhelming urge to have something to take care of. I want to fix the hole in that barn, but know that's beyond my capabilities. I will have to find something else that needs repair.

Repairs and Reparations

I almost fell out of love with Katie once.

It happened about a week after her arrival in Willow Grove. I was on my way uptown to buy a root beer when I spotted her and Son Settles walking along the railroad tracks together. They were walking toward town, so they must have been returning from what I could only assume had been a long romantic walk.

They were holding hands. Gross. Then Son said something that made Katie laugh which was even grosser.

I put my head down and turned back around toward home.

"Tucker!" she yelled.

I kept walking.

"TUCKER GAINES!"

I turned around to see Katie let go of Son's hand and wave at me. The smile on Son's face faded.

"Tucker, wait up."

She said something to Son that I couldn't hear. He shrugged and smiled sweetly. Then he gave me a nasty scowl as soon as Katie turned her back to him and ran toward me.

"Hey, where are you going?" she asked.

"Home. I was going to Ike's to get a root beer, but I'm not thirsty anymore."

"Tucker, why are you walking so fast? Slow down. What's the rush?"

She grabbed my hand, but I yanked it away.

"Tucker, what's wrong with you?"

"Nothin's wrong with me. I just happen to know where that hand of yours has been."

She raced out front of me and stopped me, putting her hands on my chest.

"Why, Tucker Gaines, are you jealous?"

"Jealous? Of Son? Hell, no. Son Settles doesn't have anything for me to be jealous of."

"That's true, Tucker. He doesn't."

This time when she grabbed my hand, I let her hold on to it.

"Son grabbed hold of my hand and it surprised me. I didn't pull away because I didn't want to hurt his feelings."

I shrugged, but my heart was lifted.

"The only reason I even went with him in the first place is because I was bored. You were off doing something with Charlie and Son saw me jumping rope in my driveway by myself. He asked if I wanted to go for a walk down the tracks. Said he had something he wanted to show me."

"What did he show you?"

"Nothing really. He showed me that he's got a little crush on me, I suppose. Kind of gave me the creeps to tell you the truth."

We walked back to Katie's house and talked until her mom called her in for dinner. As I was leaving, I saw Son Settles leaning up against a tree across the street. He spit on the ground in front of him and gave me a smile that was an insult to smiles everywhere.

He walked across the street so slowly that it confused me into not running away.

"I sure hope you ain't got designs on Katie. You see, I kinda set my sights on her."

"I don't know what you're talking about, Son. But it seems to me that Katie can make up her own mind about things."

He slugged me in the gut. I doubled over and fell to the ground as quietly as I could, not wanting Katie to see me getting my ass kicked.

"Reckon you're right, Pecker. We can all make up our own minds. You made up your mind to smart mouth me and I made up my mind to punch ya for it."

Walking away, he said, "I surely hope that Katie is better at making up her mind about things than you are, Pecker. Bad decisions have consequences, don't they?"

I would have given him a smart-ass answer in reply, but I hadn't caught my breath yet. Which was an answer unto itself.

***

I spend the better part of the day painting those sun porch stairs. Chipping away old dead flakes, brushing everything clean, and applying a thick first coat of barn-red. It's a full day's work, but with my choking dream looming, I'm not anxious to sleep again. So after dinner I walk down to Mustang's Bar & Grill for a nightcap.

Tonight, there are three patrons inside Mustang's. Two sit next to each other on the far right side and one sits alone in the center—the seat closest to the taps. There are small flickering TVs at either end of the bar and a third one above a booth in the far corner of the room. I settle into the barstool that's closest to the door.

"So what are we drinking tonight, Pecker?"

I don't recognize the voice, but I recognize the "pecker." I lift my eyes to see an older version of a face I once knew. A sparse, light-colored handlebar mustache frames the small, pursed mouth. Chewing tobacco packed tight under the lower lip, a tattered LA Dodgers baseball cap on his head. Part Yankee, all rebel, both shining bright in those intense gray-blue eyes of Son Settles.

I offer my best olive-branch smile and say, "Hey, Son. That's not the same cap, is it?"

This gets a laugh out of him. At least I think it's a laugh. It sounds a little like "Shut your white-collared, book-learning mouth, Pecker."

"No. Not the same hat."

A big fat silence follows, during which Son stands tall behind the bar, hands on hips and looks at me hard. I look back at him even harder, though I can see where to Son it might look as though I'm just staring at my feet and squirming on my stool.

"Well," I say, lifting my head again, "I am sorry about that hat, Son. Probably should have said that a long time ago."

"No worries," he says. "Pecker."

"Vodka tonic, please."

If Son Settles had ever been a friend of mine, it was just barely. I carry some of the fault for that. Things might have been different with Son and me had I not thrown his LA Dodger cap in the toilet the first time we met. Charlie Skinner had brought Son over to my house that summer afternoon, and despite the fact that he was two years older than me, I was not intimidated by Son in the least. We talked baseball, and when we started debating—"my team can beat up your team"—I told him I was going to take his Dodger cap off his head and flush it down the toilet. When he dared me to do it, do it I did.

Looking back on this, I see something in myself that has always been there: I hated the notion that someone might find me predictable.

When Son pulled his Dodger's cap out of the toilet and shook it dry, he had a look of utter astonishment on his sun-browned face. Beneath that was another look, a sort of calm-before-the-storm expression that I would come to see time and again in the years to follow—usually right before a random ass-kicking. I guess being unpredictable was important to Son, too.

We talk a little bit that night, Son and I. It isn't a bygones-be-bygones conversation, but it's nostalgic and it's nice and we laugh a time or two. It occurs to me that Son and I had indeed been friends. Just friends who didn't like each other much. It's hard to have enemies in a town like Willow Grove. You couldn't afford to.

***

Late in that night, I have the choking dream again. Except it's different this time. This time, there's an actual nightmare and I remember it. It's one of those mind-working-overtime dreams where separate realities fuse together. Where the sleeping intellect tries to make sense where sense has not been found.

Tammy is crying in agony. Her cries are coming from a room at the end of a darkened corridor. I'm in a hospital, and our child is in danger.

I sprint down the hallway, but the floor is icy slick, and I can't keep my balance. I slip and slide, tumble and fall, rise and run again. Except now the corridor rotates slowly like I'm inside a cement mixer. Tammy's cries continue to pour out from that distant room as I inch forward. I realize then that her guttural wails are coming from the room at the end of the corridor and darkness shines from that room. Like the light at the end of the tunnel, except the exact opposite.

Tammy's voice grows louder, shrill screams piercing. "Stay away from him! Keep your hands off my son!"

I turn the corner of the room, and the first thing I see is myself sitting in a rocking chair in the corner. Like some child's toy left in a disturbingly awkward pose. A mannequin with a face of exaggerated features carved on petrified wood. Bright red cheeks, bulging eyes with long lashes and thick frowning brows. Mouth and lips carved into a frozen wicked sneer. Suddenly, mannequin-me jerks his head toward real-me and locks his eyes on mine. I find contempt in his eyes.

I turn and see Tammy on a gurney; a man in doctor's scrubs stands on the other side of the cart, bent over her torso. At first, it looks as though the man has no arms, but then I realize both of his arms are wriggling deep inside of Tammy's stomach, as though trying to reverse the sleeves of an inside-out sweater. His arms fish through the insides of her abdomen and she writhes in spasms, but there's no blood. Then, with a violent jerk, he pulls both hands out. Tammy deflates before my eyes, and the man stands bolt upright. Arms extended, he holds a silent child out in front of him.

For the first time, the man looks at me, and I recognize him but cannot make out the face. I know him; I don't know him. Both hands are around Ethan's neck and the man turns him so that I might see Ethan's face. Except that it's not Ethan's face, but rather it was the face of Katie Cooper. And then the man with the face I do and do not know smiles a razor blade smile and winks.

***

My background mind has been quietly obsessing on something that the rest of me can't put my finger on. I try to walk it out of me and find my feet leading me to the playground. Swinging Girl is not here today. I take my place on the bench and behold the world of Willow Grove. There was a time when I thought this place was the world.

"Hey."

Somehow Swinging Girl has managed to sneak onto her swing without me noticing. She blows a big pink bubble that nearly conceals her entire face.

"Hello," I say. "You sure must like swinging."

"Yep. Don't you?"

I think about the porch swing at Grandma's. "Yes. I do like swinging."

The chains on her swing clang in a rhythm that gives tempo to our conversation.

"Then swing." She nods to one of the empty swings.

"Maybe next time."

"You're just going to sit there again, aren't you?"

"I've got more thinking to do."

"Have you figured out what you're even thinking about yet?"

She swings a little faster and the tempo between us picks up.

"Well, sort of. I mean, I know what I'm thinking about," I lie. "It's just … it's complicated."

"UGH!" she says, as though she has just stepped out of a Peanuts comic strip. "I hate how grown-ups are always talking about how complicated everything is."

I have no defense for that. She swings higher, faster, harder, and my heart goes with her.

"You know what's not complicated?" she asks.

"Swinging?"

She smiles and extends her legs, the tempo slowed, and for the first time, I take a real good look at her. She can't more than eleven or twelve years old—maybe younger. Freckles around her nose dot her light complexion and long lashes frame green eyes that are so light they almost look yellow. When she blinks, it conjures an image of blooming daisies in my mind.

"Didn't your parents ever tell you not to talk to strangers? There are dangerous people in the world."

"Are you dangerous?"

"No, I'm not dangerous. But nobody is going to tell you they're dangerous."

"Well, duh."

"I'm just saying, I could be dangerous. You don't know."

"I know you're not dangerous."

"How can you tell?"

"I just can. You're too sad to be dangerous."

"Listen … just humor me, ok. Tell me you don't make a habit of this."

"I don't. In fact, you are the only stranger I have ever even seen on this playground. So consider yourself humored."

I settle into the swing on the opposite end from hers. I walk it backwards, then lift my legs and glide forward. I pump until my legs stretch nearly as high as hers did, and we swing together like that, side-by-side. Not talking, not thinking, just swinging and occasionally dragging my feet to remind myself of dirt and rock and things that can be touched. After some minutes, we stop. Here we sit, twisting in our swings. The only sounds in the entire world come from the chains clanging above our heads and the gravel crunching beneath our feet. I feel her turn my way. She looks up at me with those daisies and stares hard, flower eyes dancing across my face left to right to left again, as if literally reading my face.

"Now, see, isn't that better than just sitting there?"

"Yes. It really is."

"Thought so. It's always better to do something."

Doing Something

Grandpa and Grandma are napping, though Grandpa may have been aided in the effort by a liquid sedative. I sit by myself, reading the Daily Chronicle. When I open the obituaries, which I have recently taken an interest in, my eyes are drawn to the obituary of a little girl who has recently passed.

Laura Jane Benton, 3, rural Willow Grove, died April 12th after battling a brain tumor for more than two years. She learned to walk three different times because medical battles interrupted her development, and when surgery took away her voice, she used sign language and other means to communicate. She was granted a Make-A-Wish trip to Florida where she met her favorite TV friend, Barney. Survivors include her parents Paul and Beatrice (Hart) Benton, of Willow Grove; 2 sisters, Genie and Tanya, Willow Grove; paternal Grandparents, Nicholas and Clarice Benton, Winterhaven, FL; maternal grandmother, Helen Hart, Willow Grove; maternal great grandmother, Anna Hart; 3 uncles; 1 aunt. She was predeceased by her maternal great grandfather Edmund Hart. Funeral arrangements by Anderson Funeral Home, Glidden, where memorials are established for The National Children's Cancer Society and Pediatric Brain Tumor Foundation.

Beatrice Hart had been a classmate of mine through all my school years in Willow Grove, and she'd had a crush on me through most of them. Probably because I was a little less cruel to her than most kids. Because of this, Beatrice was always giving me things—bubble gum, candy bars, even money sometimes.

As most of us grew older, Beatrice seemed to regress and withdraw. She kept to herself so much that it felt as if it literally pained her to be seen or spoken to. She looked like someone who wanted to not be noticed. When she stood, she cowered. When she spoke, her voice was muffled and the words came out garbled, as though they didn't come from her at all but rather from some smaller someone deep inside of her that strained to push the words through the barely parted lips. When she moved, it was with small steps, head tilted down so that the long, scraggly, gray-brown hair curtained her face. Nobody ever saw the eyes of Beatrice Hart.

One time in P.E., Beatrice and I had been assigned to be square-dancing partners. Her hands were clammy and as we began to dance, she was clearly nervous. After awhile, though, she did loosen up and almost seemed to be enjoying herself. I was swinging my partner round and round when my partner smiled and laughed a little bit. Then she lifted her eyes cautiously, slipping a toe into waters that were always cold for her. I yanked my hands out of hers, wiped them on my pants vigorously, and for the rest of the class we danced without touching. Without smiling. Beatrice Hart gave me a smile and I responded with a cruelty that chased it away. It should have changed me, that smile.

I wish I hadn't been so cruel. Life, I guessed, was cruel enough for Beatrice Hart.

I put down the newspaper, grab a pen and notebook, and go to the kitchen table where I write Beatrice Hart Benton a letter of apology for every cruel thing that had ever happened to her. I apologize for how unkind life had been to her and promise her my prayers. I tell her how beautiful her daughter's obituary was and how much it has moved me. How it has changed me.

I have a new hero and it is Laura Jane Benton, who demonstrated more strength and courage in her three years than most of us show in a lifetime. I promise you this, Beatrice. I will carry Laura Jane's life story with me every day for the rest of my life. It is folded up now and in my wallet.

Whenever I feel overwhelmed by life's challenges, I will read about the little girl who learned how to walk three different times. Whenever I feel weak and defeated, I will remember the little girl who learned to speak with her hands when she couldn't with her voice. Whenever I feel sorry for myself, I will pull out Laura Jane's obituary, and I will remind myself how blessed I truly I am. Whenever I feel life has been unfair to me, I will think of Laura Jane Benton who did not live to see her fourth birthday. I will also think of you, Beatrice, for life has asked more of you than it should have. And it has taken more than it has given.

I promise that I will remember you and your daughter forever. I hope it provides you some comfort to know that this world is a better place because Beatrice Hart Benton is in it. And because Laura Jane was.

I don't sign the letter and I don't mail it. Instead, I put it in an envelope and carry it to the cemetery. The Willow Grove cemetery is small and it only takes a couple minutes to locate the small patch of dirt that Laura Jane is buried beneath. I leave the letter under the angel figurine that stands where Laura Jane's headstone will soon be.

***

Some days later, I am back at the cemetery and see a different envelope sticking out from under the angel figurine, and I know it's meant for me.

I have a new friend, and it's Whoever You Are, who demonstrated more empathy and compassion than even my own family. Thank you for your letter and the promises you made. Please keep them. I do not know who you are, so I will pretend you are an angel.

Maybe I can be an angel for someone else someday. I will try to be.

With Love,

Beatrice

That hole inside me begins to fill, and it occurs to me that perhaps the baby girl in my dream wasn't Katie Cooper, but rather Laura Jane. Now that I know the meaning of my dream, hopefully it will go away.

It does not. My dreams choke me awake again that very night.

***

When I can't get back to sleep, I go downstairs to the kitchen. I am sticky with sweat, and where my heart should be, a fist tries to punch its way out of me. Or it's pounding on something inside of me that doesn't belong there.

I pull down the bottle of Scotch that Grandpa Gaines keeps above the refrigerator.

"Make it two," I hear from behind me as I pull a glass out of the cupboard.

I turn around to see Grandpa standing in the doorway. His hands are in the pockets of a gray tattered housecoat, which hang over flannel pajamas and a potbelly. I never understood how those skinny little bird legs of his could support such a heavy upper frame. It always scared me when Grandma told me how much I looked like Grandpa had when he was a younger man, because as an older man he looks like a damn ostrich.

"Sorry, I didn't mean to wake you. I thought I was being pretty quiet."

"Oh, you didn't wake me. I was up."

When I raise my eyebrows in question, he says, "We've all got our demons that keep us awake, Tuck."

He gives me a conspirator's wink. I pull down another glass and pour.

"To demons," I say, handing the glass to Grandpa.

"To demons," he returns with another wink.

We take the bottle and our empty glasses to the table and sit. I pour two more shots.

"You know," he says, "I myself never did see anything wrong with dousing one's demons with some holy spirits now and again. At the very least, you'll confuse them a little. Disorient them and get them back on their heels. If you're lucky, maybe you'll drown them altogether." He slams down his shot as though he has a fire inside him to put out.

"Here's the thing, Tuck. One way or the other, demons will change you. They can change you for the worse or they can change you for the better. You could look at the bad that's happened and try to make some good out of it. Or you could look at it and start thinking that the world owes you something, like you've got some sort of free pass."

I drink my shot and refill. "Were you ever able to drown the demons that came after Uncle Joe died?"

My Uncle Joe—Grandpa and Grandma's youngest child—had died in a car accident when he was eighteen. It was the first time I had ever brought up Joe with Grandpa, and whatever he was about to say would be the first words I ever heard him speak about the dead uncle I never knew. His own dead son.

Grandpa stares at the empty glass twisting in his hands before finally tilting it toward me. I pour, and he drinks.

"Yeah, Joe," the words escape him like a breath he's been holding for near thirty years. "No, Tuck, I've never been able to drown those demons. Joe's death did not change me for the better."

"What was he like?"

Grandpa is still focused on that empty glass, as though all his answers are sitting somewhere inside of it. He smiles out of the corner of his mouth and suppresses a laugh. "Joe was a big dumb kid, you know. Always a dumb kid. Having fun, joking around, laughing and smiling. Everyone wanted to hang around with Joe. I can still see that goofy grin of his." He finds it in the bottom of that twisting glass. Finally, he looks up at me. "Nothing ever got him down, you know? You ever know one of those people? The kind of person that always finds the good wherever they're at? Well, that was Joe all right. Except he didn't just find the good, he brought it with him. Wherever he went, he brought the good. That was Joe. That was my boy." He dabs at his eyes with the sleeves of his housecoat. "Look at me. It's been thirty years for Christ's sake."

I pour two more drinks. He sniffs and shakes his head. "Anyway, I figure when he died, he took all the good with him there, too. Wherever that might be."

"Seems to me he left some good behind, too," I say.

Grandpa stares at me hard and then downs his drink. He sets the glass down and weakly, brokenly, pushes away from the table.

"Come on," he says. "Let's go back to bed. The demons are gone for now."

***

The morning after my night of Scotch and demons with Grandpa, I walk to the Willow Grove Cemetery, which rests about a half-mile west of town. I stop first at Ethan's grave and sit on the ground behind his headstone. Exactly where I had stood with my hands on his coffin until forced to let go and watch as they lowered it into the open-mouth of the hungry earth. I would never be that close to him again. I would never be closer than these six feet. Never farther than closed eyes and a quiet moment.

"I love you, Ethan. Daddy loves you forever."

Katie Cooper's gravesite is thirty feet or so from Ethan's—from mine, too, for that matter, as my name was inscribed on one side of Ethan's, Tammy's on the other. I sat on the ground in front of Katie's headstone, put my hands to the ground, and stared at the words on the headstone.

Beloved Daughter
Katie Cooper
1969-1981

I remember every moment with Katie all at once. I close my eyes and picture her face. See it, like one of those scenes in a movie where some-one is remembered to music. *Seasons in the Sun* plays in my mind. Katie fades into shadow and when she comes back to light it is the face of Swinging Girl. She smiles her knowing smile then fades to shadow again. When Katie's face returns, she is tilting her head to one side and pulling long, wind-blown hair away from mouth and eyes. Whether I'm

Imagining or remembering, I can't say. I opened my eyes and read the headstone again.

***

1981—far away and getting farther. How many eyes had looked upon these engravings over the years? The long hard stares of friends and family wearing away the letter and number grooves. How many hearts had mourned here? More than just the Coopers and me, I hope. We can't do it all by ourselves. Between what's to remember and what's to wonder about, the three of us can't bear the load on our own.

At that moment, a familiar car pulls into the cemetery. A long silver Lincoln Continental that I recognize from the church parking lot. It drives right in front of me and then slows to a stop on the far side of the cemetery. Soon, Phyllis Ross emerges. I wave, but she doesn't see me. She pulls a spade and a colorful arrangement of wildflowers out of the trunk of the car and carries it to a nearby headstone. For the next several minutes, Phyllis does the meticulous work of planting those flowers by the grave of her deceased husband PJ. She works quietly, effortlessly. After tenderly tamping down the earth around the flowers, she returns the spade to the trunk of the car and brings back a water pail, which she fills at a nearby pump. After watering the flowers, she brushes off her knees, washes her hands, and shakes them dry. In front of the grave, with hands clasped together loosely—back bent from the years it carried and the burdens it bore—she looks down with the warm smile that she'd been wearing all along. When she leaves, I go over to PJ's headstone.

Beloved Husband and Father
Peter Ross, Jr. "PJ"
1911-1995

Beloved. There it was again. That was the thing, wasn't it? Daughter, husband, father, whatever. Year of birth, year of death, the dash in-between. If you were beloved, then, man, you had done something, hadn't you? I thought about Beatrice Hart and her little girl Laura Jane, whose obituary was folded inside my wallet. That little girl who hadn't lived to see the age of four had changed me forever. And so had PJ Ross who had lived to eighty-four. Once beloved, always beloved.

I head back to Grandpa and Grandma's to make more repairs to the hole in my barn. And to try to make myself more beloved.

***

… he didn't vomit, but for a minute there, he was sure he was going to. The longer Tucker had stood at Katie's grave, the more convinced he was that Katie was telling secrets from the grave. He half expected Tucker to wheel around and look right at him accusingly. His heart pounded with the anticipation of this. What would he do if that were to happen? What if Tucker somehow discovered the secret? To what lengths would the monster go to make sure the secret died there? With Tucker …

***

I have a pen, a notebook, and a vodka tonic. The paper remains blank until I figure out that what I actually need is a pen, a notebook, and *two* vodka tonics. But it's the third drink that loosens the lid on my emotions and the fourth that pops it off. I tilt my head back in my chair, closed my eyes, and let the vodka remember what it wants to remember. Let it feel what it wants to feel. The past swirls before me, and I write. I think about good old PJ and jot down the memories that come. Coaching my park district baseball team when I was six. Greeting me with a handshake and a warm smile every time he saw me in church. How he could click a little wink at you and make you feel like he knew you inside and out and liked you anyway. *It's okay. We all make mistakes. I like you. You're a good person.* I picture him bouncing along on his John Deere tractor out in his fields of corn. Planting in the spring, harvesting in the fall. I think of that old tractor sitting in a dark barn, covered with cobwebs and buried in dust. As un-living as old PJ himself, and rightly so.

By my fourth vodka tonic, I have managed to put words to the slideshow in my head. I carefully fold the letter with sharp even creases and slide it into an envelope that I do not seal. I can't wait for morning. I leave right then and there and again walk the half-mile to that dark and lifeless lot. Old Man Moon lights my path, and I'm able to find PJ fairly easily. I stand in front of the headstone with my hands clasped together in front of me the same way that Phyllis had earlier that same day. Then I pull the envelope out of my back pocket and paper clip it to receptive flowery fingers.

***

I go to the cemetery every day that week. Talk to Ethan and Katie, and keep watch on the letter I have left for Phyllis. By Saturday afternoon, it is gone, and so Sunday morning, I go to church just to see if Phyllis Ross looks different somehow.

The last time I had been inside the Willow Grove United Methodist Church was for my son's funeral. My breath quickens at the sight of the emptiness that fills the space where Ethan had lay in his coffin. The same kind of emptiness I saw occupying the hole in that barn.

Mom and Larry aren't here this Sunday, so I sit by myself in the spot that Grandma Mueller used to sit in every Sunday. She is to be credited for this flat and faded cushion, having worn it down one Sunday at a time.

The congregation is smaller as membership growth has been outpaced by attrition. Attrition by life that carried youngsters away from home. Attrition by death that carried the elderly farther than that.

When Pastor Judy asks the congregation to share their joys and concerns, several hands shoot up. Alice Todd asks for prayers for our military overseas. Elmer and Millie Sands announce the birth of their nineteenth grandchild. Florence Howell gives thanks for the sun. A part of me was hoping that Phyllis would raise her hand and tell the congregation about her grave letter. She does not, however, and it saddens me because my joy is all wrapped up in hers.

Pastor Judy leads us in a long passionate prayer, full of high praises, sincere gratitude, and humble requests. I close my eyes to add power to the prayer, but my mind drifts back to those Sundays when I would sit here next to Grandma Mueller and she would scratch secret messages on my back with loving fingers. *Hi, T. Love you, T. My boy.*

When Pastor Judy has finished, she encourages everyone to take a few seconds for silent personal prayer, so I thank God for my wife and daughter and ask for more feathers.

I don't know that I get much from being here. I listen for messages but don't find any in sermon or song. Still, just being seems to calm my soul a little.

***

… it's a Sunday morning, which means most of the citizens of Willow Grove are either in bed, in church, or in the fields. Nobody was ever around at this time on a Willow Grove Sunday. If a person were inclined to criminal behavior, this would be the time for it. Nobody around at all … other than that one little bundle of sugar and spice on a playground swing. And one little monster …

***

In the fellowship hall after the service, I'm listening to Albert Todd talk about how the Church Trustees Committee is in search of a back-up generator *so if you know anybody who has one or wants to donate one or …* when, from behind me, a dramatic Phyllis Ross tells her friends Sally Coleman and Carol Carney about the "wonderful letter" someone had left by PJ's grave. I swallow my donut hole and choke down the rest of the last bit of the ridiculously strong decaffeinated coffee in my Styrofoam cup. I feign an increasing interest in Albert's generator talk, but back myself into a position where I can better eavesdrop on Phyllis and friends.

"Goodness, how lovely. Who was it from?" asked Carol.

"Well that's the thing," Phyllis answered. "It wasn't signed."

Sally gasps.

"It wasn't signed?" Carol whispers. "Oh my, an anonymous letter."

"At the bottom of the letter it said, *He won't be forgotten.*"

I shift a half-turn on my feet and can see them out of the corner of my eye. I nod toward Albert, but fine-tune my ears into the ladies' conversation. Carol and Sally pepper Phyllis with questions from the left and the right. Breathy and desperate, they gasp out their speculations. All at once it seems important. I feel like part of something bigger than my curiosity and lighter than my grief. I know something they don't. There's an odd power to it. They continue guessing, shooting out names like firecrackers on the fourth of July until they begin to run out of steam.

"What do you think, Phyllis?" Sally asks.

Phyllis sounds dubious. "I don't know. This doesn't seem like anything these folks would do."

"Well, who then?"

***

After church and still feeling spiritual, I walk up the playground. But I'm almost relieved to find that Swinging Girl is not there. I was starting to feel weird about our relationship and she wasn't, which concerned me.

So I leave the playground and head out to the cemetery to visit Ethan. Tammy had not wanted our son buried here, nearly an hour from our home in Westfield. But the Gaines family plot is here and this brings me some measure of comfort. I should not have insisted, I suppose. I should have let her keep him as close to her as possible, but I did not.

It is so much warmer today than it had been on the day of his funeral. And so quiet. I lie down flat on my stomach and my heart beats against the earth and back again against my chest. As if it is Ethan's beating back at me, or just the one heart we are sharing for a moment. Somebody once said having children is like letting your heart live outside your body. Yeah, it's exactly like that.

To live in the hearts we leave behind is not to die

That is the quote we put on the back of Ethan's headstone. I close my eyes and try to feel him living there inside me, but the truth is that it feels almost like the opposite. Like something that had once been there is now missing.

I wipe away tears and pull a blade of grass from above his resting place and tuck it inside my sock against the angel tattooed there. "I love you, Ethan. Daddy loves you forever."

Mr. Innocent

I see and recognize Charlie Skinner the instant I step into Mustang's Bar and Grill. I'm not sure how I am able to so quickly recognize someone I haven't seen in well over ten years, but I do. Maybe it's his slouch—even more pronounced than my own. Like some street urchin, hunched over and enclosed within himself to protect his last warm thing—the beating heart inside his chest. He's propped up on a barstool, elbows on the bar and an empty glass in front of him.

For a long time Charlie Skinner was my best friend. He might even still count as the best friend I've ever had if such rankings are based on Wiffle ball games played, imaginary bad guys killed, and giggles. Man, could we make each other laugh.

But there was a marker that had ended my friendship with Charlie the same way that the carbon engine had ended the horse and buggy. It was the arrival of Katie Cooper.

"Yep."

"Well, filler up for me would ya, Stan?" he says to the bartender I am not familiar with. Son Settles must have the night off.

Stan the bartender returns moments later with a full glass. There are only four other patrons in the tavern. The only one I know is Old Man Keller who is sitting at the table behind Charlie and hovering over a glass of something dark and icy. Strange to see the Old Man sitting atop anything other than that mower. Like seeing a cop out of uniform.

I remain standing just inside the door trying to decide whether I want to turn back around and go home or sit on the stool next to Charlie. There are no other options.

"Is this seat taken?" I ask.

Without turning his head, Charlie says, "Depends." And then he sips the foam off the top of his draught and sighs. "You aren't going to make me eat grass, are you?"

Charlie and I used to wrestle around a lot when we were kids. There were a few times that things got heated and I would pin him down, rip grass from the ground and shove it between his lips with prying fingers until he surrendered and opened wide. It was such a ridiculous form of torment that invariably we both laughed ourselves out of our rage. At least that's how I remember it.

"You were always stronger than me. Why did you let me do that?" I ask.

"Because you were always angrier." He motions down to the bartender that I need a drink. "Put it on my tab, Stan."

"That's okay, I'll get it," I protest.

"Stan, put it on my tab," he repeats in such a way that Stan will not question further. In such a way that told me that Charlie had heard about Ethan, which was as close as we'd come to actually talking about him.

Charlie and I have the "how ya doin'" and "whatcha been up to" conversations. We have the "remember that time" laughs. We talk about our families without digging below the surface of name, rank, and serial number. And we dance around how we had drifted apart and how different we really were back then, or explore how different we are now. Sitting on the bar in front of him is a panama hat. I was going to ask him about it, but thought better of it. Wearing a weird hat is the kind of thing you do when you want the world to think of you in a way they hadn't before. That's all I really need to know.

"You see much of Moose anymore? Whatever came of him?"

"I don't see any more of Moose Thornton than you see of Katie Cooper," he replies.

I let the beer swish around in my mouth as the words swish around in my head. I slowly swallow everything.

"What does that mean?"

"It means that Moose has been dead for about seven or eight years now. Was hot-rodding in town on his Harley when some old blue-hair ran a Yield sign and pulled out in front of him on south 3rd."

"Jesus. Were you there when it happened?"

"I was. Moose flew over the top of that friggin' Buick and skidded about 200 feet. Blood and brains halfway down 3rd Street. Dead. Just like that."

He says this last part with an emphatic snap of his fingers. He drains the rest of his beer and motions to Stan for two more.

"The old lady stopped in shock, looked over at Moose lying there, looked at us and raced off at about twenty miles per hour. Not a whole lot of 'run' in her 'hit-and-run'."

"Who was it?"

"I don't know. Some out-of-towner on a visit. She could have took off at a hundred-and-twenty and it wouldn't have made a difference. Nothing happens in Willow Grove that somebody doesn't see or know about."

"Again, like Katie."

He sits silent for a moment and then cocks his head as if to consider something. Then gazing straight ahead, he says, "No, not like Katie Cooper."

"What do you mean?"

"You talkin' about the guy who supposedly saw Katie with ol' Slim Jim by the railroad tracks?"

"Yeah."

"Never happened." He shakes his head and gives a dismissive wave of the hand.

"What are you talking about?"

"I'm talking about that night she was found. I'm not even sure there ever was an *anonymous tip*. And even if there was, I don't believe any-*body* saw any-*thing*."

The day that Katie went missing, the entire town had searched for her. Then, early the next morning, an anonymous tipster had called the

Sheriff's Office to say that they had seen a transient who had come to town a few weeks earlier walking down the railroad tracks with Katie. It was that tip that led the Sheriff to Katie's body.

"Why do you say that?"

"Because while the whole town was out looking for Katie that night, Moose and I was drinking a six-pack behind the lumberyard and saw that hobo Slim Jim come loafing by 'bout eleven o'clock. We sat and watched that goofy SOB walk through the Halpern's backdoor and come right back out about five minutes later with a jar of peanut butter, a spoon, and a gallon of milk."

Sticking my fingers in my ears to clear out the wax would be cliché, but that's what I feel like doing.

"Are you telling me that Slim Jim was innocent of murder because he was guilty of stealing?"

"Kind of funny when you say it like that—ironic like."

He laughs and takes a swig of beer before continuing.

"Gaines, you gotta ask yourself … does that sound like the behavior of a man who had killed a little girl? Even Slim Jim—dumbass that he was—would have known enough to get the hell out of Dodge. Instead he goes for a midnight snack?"

Behind Charlie, Old Man Keller orders another Jack Daniels and Coke then pays us a greeting.

"Hey boys, how ya doin' this evening?"

"Fine, thanks. Yourself?" I ask.

"Can't complain. Another day above ground."

Stan places the Jack and Coke in front of him and Keller snatches it up in greedy little grass-stained hands. He turns back toward his table and lifts his glass in a toast.

"You boys be good now."

With the Old Man back at his table, I shift my attention back to Charlie

"Why didn't the Halperns ever report anything?"

"Report what? A missing gallon of milk? They probably never even noticed. Slim Jim walked into a dark house and walked out of a dark house."

The door front slams shut behind me as unknown patron number one leaves the bar. I peek over at Keller who is coddling his drink and chomping on ice. The Old Man smiles and nods.

"Why didn't you and Moose tell Sheriff Buck?"

"Now, that's a fair question. I actually thought about it. I did," he says with a rehearsed nod. "But Moose talked me out of it. We would have caught ourselves some serious licks for sneaking out and drinking like that. Hell, we were only, what, thirteen? Plus Moose said that Slim Jim still could have done it and we'd be risking our necks for some psychopath who we already knew for sure was at least one kind of criminal."

I imagine the entire scene in my head, trying to make sense of it. I can see Moose and Charlie leaning up against that old lumberyard shed, drinking Old Milwaukee or Pabst Blue Ribbon or whatever they could get their underage hands on. Along comes Slim Jim, walking under the moonlight in his torn pants and blue-jean jacket.

"Why wouldn't you guys have called him over when you saw him? He was your buddy, you hung out with him earlier that very day, didn't you?"

"Well, for one we figured he would have wanted some of our beer. For two, playing with Ol' Creepy in the park in broad daylight is one thing. Hidden behind that barn at night is something different altogether. Especially *that night*."

So Charlie and Moose had watched everything. Everything that happened that night and the days that followed. And they knew.

"I know I should have said something. Even knew it then. But it was easier not to. And with every day that passed, it got easier. An easy decision to make, a hard secret to keep. Know what I mean? Like something heavy was hung on me that night and I've walked with it ever since. Shit, you realize that up until this very moment Moose and I were the only two who had ever known that secret? And for the past seven years it's been mine alone."

He drained his beer.

"Hell, I feel a little bit lighter already."

"I don't know, man. It doesn't add up. Why would someone lie about seeing Slim Jim that day? It doesn't make sense."

"I don't know, Gaines. I guess you gotta ask yourself what motivates a man to say something he know ain't true. No reward. No glory really. What was in it for him?"

He motions for Stan to bring another round of drinks over.

"And let me throw one other thing at ya there, Gaines. You know that Slim Jim is RIPing out in the Willow Grove cemetery, right?"

"No, I didn't know that, but so what?"

"So, he died in prison. He didn't have any friends or family to claim his body—not here in Willow Grove anyway. The only way he gets a plot and a tombstone in Willow Grove is if somebody pays to bring his body back here and pay for the burial. Would take a person feeling a whole lot of sympathy to do something like that."

"Or someone feeling a whole lot of guilt."

"Exactly."

Stan sets down two more beers in front of us.

"On the tab, Stan," Charlie says as he rises from his bar stool. "I've gotta hit the head. Maybe you'll have the mystery solved by the time I get back, Sherlock."

For the two hours that followed, Charlie and I made like we were best friends once again. After all the talk of Katie and Slim Jim, we returned to the comforts of *remember when* and *whatever happened to so and so*. We laughed and slapped each other on the shoulders, but Katie Cooper was walking around in the back of my mind the entire time.

As I walk home in my drunken stupor, I feel heavy. Heavier than the alcohol. Heavy like that secret that Charlie had hung around my neck. If Slim Jim didn't kill Katie, who did? And what would have led someone to pay for his burial if not the gnawing guilt of a killer's conscious?

Still echoing through some back corner of my mind was another question. The question that Swinging Girl had asked me that very first day in the park.

What are you doing here?

I was starting to think the answer to that question was much different than I had originally thought. Like this trip wasn't about Ethan at all. Like it was about Katie Cooper.

I'm on my way to moving on, but the moving on comes slow
And I can't get past the gettin' past cause the gettin' past won't go
I'm just walking down this old dirt path that keeps on circlin' round
And when I take two steps forward only one foot hits the ground.

One foot walks with Satan and one walks with the Son
And I'm right there in between holding hands with either one
One may walk on fire and flame or one may walk on cloud
But wherever I may be walkin' it's with one foot on the ground.

I've got a heart that flies with angels and a soul that bears the load
Of a mind that keeps me human, keeps me reaping what I have sowed
I've got an angel-scar on my left leg and he steps in silent sound
But wherever he may take me, I keep that right foot on the ground.

One foot walks with sinners and one foot walks with saints
And while one foot walks the skies above, one's tied down with chains
My angel-scar he guides me, keeps me moving Heaven-bound
But his wings will never lift me while this right foot's on the ground.

When Mom and Dad got married, Grandpa and Grandma gave them this house as a wedding gift. They had raised their children in this home and now their children's children would be raised here as well. When my parents divorced eleven years later, Grandpa and Grandma bought it back from them. This was The House of Gaines, after all. In the years that I had lived here, nothing new had gone up and nothing old had come down. It was a place and time frozen in state, perfectly preserved like some ice-age victim woolly mammoth. There wasn't a stone I hadn't kicked or a tree I hadn't climbed. I knew every house on every street and every person in every house.

And then Katie Cooper came along and I—like some overbearing island tour guide—took it upon myself to show Katie the ins and outs of the town. I walked her downtown to the United Methodist Church and let her know that the Sunday service started at nine a.m. I told her how the Corwin's was the place to go when you were hungry and your mom wouldn't give you a snack because Mrs. Corwin always offered visitors apple pie or almond cookies or buns fresh from the oven and still warm. I showed her every hidden path and every shortcut and warned her about the unfriendly people like Lyle Weber and Abigail Simpson, who would holler at you if they caught you cutting through their yard.

On the last day of our tour, I took her to the train tracks where I made a big production out of digging around in my pockets for change. Truth was, I had exactly two coins in my pocket—each a shiny new copper penny.

"Here you go," I said holding it out. "A brand new penny. See, it says 1981 right on it. Mine does, too."

"Neat," she said. "What are we going to do with them?"

"You'll see."

I bent down and pressed my ear against the cold rail and Katie did the same.

"Hear that?"

"Yes, what is it?"

"A train."

We hopped up, laid our pennies on the tracks, and waited for the big yellow dragon to thunder through with its fire of roars and whistles.

When it did, it left two squashed and warm keepsakes in its wake. I handed one to her.

"Here, don't lose it."

"What do we do with them?" she asked.

"Nothing. You just keep them."

"Oh, you mean like a souvenir?

"Yeah, like a souvenir. Or a friendship thing."

"Cool! I'll keep it forever."

"Put it somewhere safe."

"Come on," she said. "I should probably go home."

The tour had ended. There was nothing else that I could offer Katie Cooper. I'd shown her everything I knew.

When I got home that evening, I put that penny in my Treasure Box (an old shoebox I kept hidden under my bed) along with some other of my most prized possessions: a wristwatch with my name inscribed on the face of it, postcards from traveling friends and family, a Buffalo Nickel, and few other odds and ends.

I found out later that Katie ended up losing her penny. I had always meant to get her another one, but never got the chance.

***

A few days later it was Katie who was revealing secrets of this town to me.

"Come on, I want to show you something."

She tugged me along, though I was anything but reluctant. Katie led me to the train tracks and we walked them west out of town.

She wore a large, wide-brimmed garden hat that I had not seen before and it made her seem older. The hat should have looked ridiculous on her and it probably did to any other beholder, but not to me. To me, it glimpsed the future and I imagined how nice it would be to someday walk by her side with my own silly hat. For whatever reason, the hat was a sombrero and I daydreamed of a mustachioed future-me walking hand-in-hand with Katie on my right and my donkey on my left. I giggled.

"What's so funny?"

I glanced at her hat and quickly looked away.

"Are you laughing at my hat?" she said aghast, pulling the sides down over her ears. The only way she could have looked cuter in that moment was if she were holding a wet puppy.

"What? No! I was just … I was just remembering something funny, that's all."

"Don't you lie to me, Tucker Gaines, you were laughing at my hat and I know it. You think I look silly."

I felt my face flush and I knew that with Katie there would never be a secret I could keep or a lie I could tell.

"No, Katie, you don't look silly. It's just one more kind of way you look pretty."

It was very 'aw-shucks' and I surprised myself by saying it.

She stopped in her tracks and turned to me. Her eyes were wider and greener than I had ever seen them and she had a look of all smiles and all tears. She kissed me on the cheek and suddenly I felt all smiles and all tears myself, which confused me.

"Katie, I'm going to marry you some day."

I said it because I didn't know what else to say in that moment. I also said it because I meant it. More earnest words I would never speak.

She did not respond, but there was something like bliss to the look she gave me. She sniffed, lowered her head, and wiped her nose on a rolled-up sleeve. Then she grabbed my hand.

"Come on. We're almost there."

She led me back through a dense thicket of bushes and shrubs that didn't scratch or scrape as we passed through. Like background music, summer made its sounds for us. Tweets and chirps from above, whistles and croaks from around.

Once through the undergrowth, we stopped and she handed me her hat. I followed her through waist-high grass and then she stopped, turned and faced me.

"Close your eyes."

She squeezed my hand and a tingle shivered through the whole of me. I decided that I could probably give up sight forever if this was the trade-off.

"Almost there. No peeking."

We stepped forward and dewy leaves brushed my face. I passed from light to shade, from hot to temperate.

"Ta-da!" she said with a wave of her wrist. "Open your eyes."

And when I did, what I saw was so beautiful it actually frightened me—because what I was seeing was so unfamiliar to me and so improbable to Willow Grove that I seriously questioned whether it was heaven.

I thought back on my day, but couldn't remember dying.

What was this place and how could I not know of it? This was *my* town. It was so picturesque that if I had seen an apple and a serpent you could have convinced me we had stepped into the Garden of Eden. There was a small pond with dark waters that reflected the splendors of nature that surrounded it. Plants and flowers I did not recognize. Colors I did not even seen before. Sounds that must have been music. Music that danced across me until it seeped through my skin and was soaked up by my insides.

"Where are we? How did you find this place? When—I mean, when did you even have time?"

We had been together almost every day since Katie had moved to town two weeks prior and already I had fallen deep within the spell of her charm. I was spending more and more time with Katie, less and less with Charlie. We took long walks and had longer conversations where we told each other all of our most favorite things and then all of our least. I told her what pests my brother and sister were and she told me how she wished she had brothers and sisters. That it was better to be pestered than lonely.

Sometimes we would entertain each other with lies and stories, spoken in foreign accent and whispered with dramatic flair. We conversed under tented-blankets, high in trees, lying in the grass amongst a field of dandelions. We shared secrets, made promises, and laughed at the silliness of boys and girls. And now this. This Garden of Willow Grove.

We stole away to this secret place every chance we could. To splash in the pond. To be still in the grasses. To be together. Katie was sweet and kind and good. Good like the fishes of the seas and the birds of the sky. Good like Eve before the apple.

Katie Cooper was the greatest good I ever knew.

***

The same summer that Katie Cooper came to Willow Grove, a tall thin transient we came to know as Slim Jim also drifted into town. The first time I saw Slim Jim, he was playing with Jeff and Mary Jo Welp. I thought he must be a visiting uncle or something, because I had never seen him before. Mary Jo was on top of Slim Jim's shoulders and Jeff was chasing them around the yard. He caught them and they all tumbled and rolled around on the ground together in laughter.

A couple days later, Katie and I were playing outside when Slim Jim again showed up at the Welp's. This time, there were three or four other kids from the neighborhood, including Charlie

Katie and I watched from the other side of the street as Slim Jim and the other neighborhood kids played tag. Slim Jim seemed to be the main target to be "it," and he was an easy target, as he did not run fast. Not because he was slow, but because he wanted to be caught.

After Charlie tagged him, Slim Jim chased after Mary Jo who flopped and giggled when Slim Jim wrapped his arms around her from behind and tackled her to the ground.

"I've got you now," he roared as they fell together.

And all the kids jumped on top, pushing and pulling at Slim Jim to free Mary Jo from his grasp.

When the laughter subsided, Slim Jim looked over at Katie and me. His eyes darted back and forth between us, but finally settled on me and he asked me my name.

I shrugged my shoulders.

"Tucker!" my friends all shouted.

Standing up, he brushed himself off and finger-combed the top of his head, fixing the left-to-right part in his hair. There was a hole in his jeans at his left knee and his grimy white t-shirt was half-tucked, half-untucked. He must have been six-foot-two, but was thin and not physically intimidating. His eyes seemed unnaturally wide open, the right one more so than the left, and his lips were parted in a perpetual smile. He had a neighborly quality about him. Almost Mr. Rogers neighborly. He stuck out his hand in a gentlemanly way and introduced himself.

"Tucker, I'm Jim. Your friends here have taken to calling me Slim Jim on account of how I'm so skinny, I s'pose. Pleased to make your acquaintance."

He offered a hand and I took it.

***

We played with Slim Jim every afternoon that week. Tag, hide-and-seek, whatever. He never came and he never went, always wore the same tattered clothes. As I was leaving at the end of that third afternoon, Slim Jim stopped me.

"Where you going, Tuck?"

"I've gotta go in for supper."

He pulled out a small fine-toothed black comb from his back pocket and combed his hair down.

"Oh, is your mom home?"

"Yeah, and she ordered a pizza. I just saw the delivery guy leave so I gotta go."

"Pizza! You lucky dog. You know how long it's been since I had pizza?"

"Do you want to eat with us? I could ask my mom?"

"You don't think she'd mind?" he asked, putting the comb back in his pocket.

"I don't know. Probably not," I said. "I'll go ask."

At home in the kitchen, I asked my mom if Slim Jim could come over for pizza.

"Who's Jim," she asked.

"A guy from the neighborhood."

Puzzled, she said, "There's no Jim in this neighborhood."

She moved the drapes aside and looked out the kitchen window. Then she turned to walk to the living room. I followed.

"Well, he doesn't live in the neighborhood, but he plays with us here. He plays with the kids in the neighborhood. He's really fun and he's nice and he hasn't had pizza for a long time."

"I don't think so, Tucker," Mom said, still walking.

"Aww, come on, Mom! He's really nice and he's fun. You'd like him."

Then she snapped, "I said no, Tu—"

She gasped and stopped in her tracks.

I turned behind me to see what her wide eyes were staring at and saw a smiling Slim Jim standing on the front porch on the other side of our screen door.

Through the door, he looked even bigger than usual. He hunched over slightly, but you still couldn't see the top of his head he was so tall. He had a hand above his brow, trying to see inside. His face was pressed up against the screen door, his face distorted like a bank robber with a nylon stocking over his head.

"Evening, ma'am," he said.

With his hair neatly combed and parted, Slim Jim had the look of a young boy whose mother had just finished licking him clean for Sunday school, but he had a grizzly growth of hair on his face and a hole on the left side of his smile

"Um, hi," she said after a moment. "You must be Jim."

"I am indeed, mam. Pleased to make your acquaintance," he said nodding his head forward and offering his right hand while his left went behind his back and held an imaginary hat.

My mother recoiled slightly but noticeably at the extended hand. She did not open the door between them.

"I'm sorry," she said holding up guilty hands, "I was just dumping the garbage and didn't get a chance to wash."

"You've got a fine boy there," he said pointing his head towards me, keeping his eyes on Mom. "Invited me in for pizza 'cause he knows I like it and that I ain't been eatin' too good lately. He said that he had to ask you first but thought you'd be fine with it. You're raising that boy right. Teaching him the right things, I mean."

He had that Slim Jim smile on his face the whole time he was talking. Except that somehow it looked different. Kind of like the "I know something you don't know" smile that my sister Heather would taunt me with whenever she had a secret.

Behind him, Old Man Keller puttered around on his Cub Cadet, cutting the Cooper's front lawn.

"Yes, thank you. We're very proud of Tucker," my mother said. "Of course, one of the things we've taught him is not to talk with strangers. I'm sure you understand."

Slim Jim chortled out a little laugh and said, "Oh, I'm not a stranger, ma'am. The whole neighborhood knows me."

The handle on the screen door started to turn downward. Slim Jim was slowly turning it from the other side. His smiling face seemed to sink back into the darkening sky behind him, like he was becoming part of it—or it a part of him.

Keller and his Cub Cadet crossed back and forth behind Slim Jim like the carriage on a typewriter. Mom reached down and grabbed the door handle from the inside, held it firm in place.

"Well, that may be, but this is the first time you and I have met. Now that we've met, though, I guess you could say that we're on our way to becoming friends."

Old Man Keller shut down the Cub Cadet and Willow Grove was silent again. I could see him talking to Katie, but the only thing I could hear was the sound of Slim Jim wheezing thick air in and out of his nose. I looked back up at him and the world around him got darker still, but in a way that was not familiar to me. Not dark like an approaching storm or a passing shadow. It was dark like doom.

Slim Jim slowly pulled his hand away from the door and shifted his stare down and to the right in a defeated manner, and then his eyes sort of jittered side-to-side real fast. The perpetual smile curled down and his nostrils flared, like an angry cry might be coming. When he lifted his head up to look at us again, he looked lost.

Then from the side of the porch came this, "I think it's time you leave, mister."

It was my Grandpa Gaines, sounding like the tough guy sheriff from some tumbleweed town in the old west. How long had he been standing there, I wondered? If I was surprised, Slim Jim was flat out shocked to hear what sounded like the voice of the law.

Grandpa had a gallon of milk and a grocery bag in his arms. He must have been on his way home from Ike' and seen Slim Jim trying to make his way in.

"That's fine. I understand. Maybe I'll come back later. Some other time, I mean."

As he turned and started to walk away, the world came out of its shadow. The Cub Cadet came back to life and grumbled home. Kids passed by on their bicycles. Life resumed. When he got to the sidewalk, Slim Jim turned back around and looked at us. Less sinister this time, he smiled sadly. Like he was sorry for things that had and had not happened. He finger-combed his hair left-to-right and winked at me.

Grandpa walked up toward the porch.

"You two all right?"

"Yes, we're fine, Hollis. Thank you," Mom said. Then turning to me she added, "I don't want you near that man again. You hear me, Tucker Gaines? He gives me the heebie-jeebies."

"I'm sure he's harmless, Tuck, but your mom is right. No need to be messin' around with some stranger passing through town. He'll be on his ways somewhere else in a couple days." And then he added with a wink, "Maybe sooner even."

That was the last time I ever talked to Slim Jim. Mom called some of the neighbors that night and warned them about the "creepy drifter" who had been playing with the kids in town.

***

My Aunt Paula—who lived two houses away from Grandpa and Grandma—had grown hydrangeas for as long as I can remember. They stood tall and beautiful at one end of what was otherwise a perennially neglected garden. But the hydrangeas required little care, which was fortunate because that's exactly what they received. And some they flourished against all odds and circumstance. Fat little flower heads bouncing and bobbing on flimsy green neck stems. Held upright by the buoyancy of their very beauty perhaps. The splendor that red and white and pink brought to an otherwise green world. As a kid, I remember thinking that Heaven must be like that. Like your whole life you know nothing but green and then you die and it's like—BAM! White! Pink! Red! It's kind of what Katie Cooper was like—the color in my world of green. Maybe it was that thought that led me to sneak out of bed past midnight and cut a few of Paula's hydrangeas to give to Katie.

Mrs. Cooper opened the door that Saturday morning to find me holding the dozen flowers I had liberated from Aunt Paula.

"Oh my," said Mrs. Cooper. She waved a dishcloth at the bee buzzing over me and said "shoo" a couple times before ushering me inside.

"Well, good morning, Tucker," said Mr. Cooper over the top of the newspaper. "What's got you up so early on a Saturday morning?" He and Katie were sitting at the kitchen table with clean plates in front of them.

"Um, nothing really," I said. Glimpsing at Katie out of the corner of my eye, I added, "Just out walking around, I guess."

"What do you have there," Mrs. Cooper asked, indicating the flowers.

"Oh, these? These are just some flowers I found while I was walking around. I found them and thought, maybe … I don't know, thought they looked nice I guess and …" Suddenly I was warm. My shoes were untied.

Mrs. Cooper jumped in. "Well, um … yes, they are beautiful. Would you like me to put them in water?"

"Yeah. Sure."

She filled a vase with water, cut the stems, and put the flowers inside. Then she put the vase on the kitchen table in front of Katie.

"There, now, that's just lovely. Don't you think so, Katie?"

"They're beautiful," said Katie, her face looking as red as mine felt.

"Why don't you have a seat, Tucker," said Mrs. Cooper. "We were about to have breakfast—pancakes and sausage."

Mr. Cooper pulled out the chair between him and Katie. Mrs. Cooper stacked our plates high with pancakes and framed the pancakes with sausage links. They asked me a lot of questions that I was proud to be able to answer. I told them about Mrs. Bianchi, who would be my and Katie's teacher in the fall. Supposedly, she was a grouch, but she graded pretty easy. I told them what hours the post office and Brenda's Hometown Café were open. I told them about my Aunt Paula the mayor-beautician and stumbled into confessing to taking the flowers from her garden.

"And if you ever need any wood or lumber or anything, you'd get that from Pease Lumber uptown. Let me know, though, because Mr. Pease's granddaughter is in my class and she likes me so I could probably get you a discount."

Mr. Cooper shot me an impressed look and said, "I'll keep that in mind."

And then he said, "What's the granddaughter's name? This girl who likes you."

"Um, Sheri, but I didn't mean that she *likes* me. We're friends is all."

"Of course, you're friends. You like each other."

"Yes," I said. Then looking at Katie, "Well, no. I mean, I don't like her."

From the stove, Mrs. Cooper said, "Howard, behave yourself."

I chanced a look over at Katie who was staring straight down into her lap and stifling a giggle.

"Tucker, your Grandparents live in town here, don't they?" asked Mrs. Cooper.

"Yep. Grandpa and Grandma Mueller both died a few years ago, but Grandpa and Grandma Gaines live three blocks away from us. He's a truck driver. Hauls cattle and pigs for the farmers around here. Mr. Patterson does, too, but Grandpa's better. He gets up real early in the morning. Also, he's real safe. His handle is "Snail" on account of how slow he drives. I don't have a handle yet, but I'll get one when I'm older and can help drive some loads for him."

"So, you're going to be a truck driver when you grow up?" asked Mr. Cooper.

"Oh, no sir," I said. "That would only be part-time. To get money for college and stuff."

"Well, then, if you're not going to be a truck driver, what are you going to be?"

I could feel my forehead and eyebrows crinkle up as I thought seriously about that question for a minute, which was about a fifty-eight seconds longer than I had ever previously spent on that question.

"Well, sir. I guess I'd like to be a baseball player, but I suppose I can't count on that. Not too many people get to do that and they don't even have baseball at the high school. So, if I can't do that, I guess maybe a writer."

"A writer? You mean like an author?"

"Yes, sir. I think I'd like to write stories and stuff. I won the Junior Writer's award for 4th grade. Plus, I've written some poems my mom says are really good."

After saying this, I snuck a look over at Katie who I found smiling widely at me.

"Poetry, huh?" said Mr. Cooper. "You mean like love poems? Stuff like that?"

"Howard, if you're done eating will you clear the table please," interjected Mrs. Cooper. "Katie, why don't you and Tucker go and play. It looks beautiful outside."

"We're in the middle of a conversation here, Betty. I was going to ask Tuck to recite some of his poetry for us. How 'bout that, Tuck, would you read us one of your poems?"

"Another time," Mrs. Cooper said. "Outside you two."

Stepping off the porch together, Katie said, "Sorry about my dad. He likes to tease is all."

"That's okay. My dad does the same thing."

"He likes you, I can tell," she said.

"Yeah?"

"Yeah. Always calling him 'sir' like you did. That's good. He likes that."

After a few minutes of walking in silence and kicking at rocks, Katie spoke up again.

"So you write poetry, huh?

"I don't know. Some, I guess."

"Can I read it?"

"Read it? Why? It's not very good."

"That's okay, I want to read it anyway. Besides, I'll bet it's a lot better than you say."

"I don't think so, Katie."

"Well, can I read it anyway?"

"I don't know."

"Oh, come on! Please!"

I squirmed, looked around, stomach turned, look at her. I couldn't believe what this little girl could get me to do.

"Promise you won't make fun?"

"Promise."

"Promise not to tell anyone?"

"Promise."

"Promise to like it?"

She squeezed my arm above the elbow.

"I already do."

***

It's hard to keep secrets in old houses, what with all the moaning and groaning they do. What with all the tattletale creaking of wooden floors and old doors swinging on cranky hinges.

Still, I manage to sneak out without waking Grandpa or Grandma Gaines.

It's well past midnight and I'm still buzzing on vodka when I step off the back porch and look up at that nosy old moon. It's low in the sky that I almost feel as if I'm looking down at it, which makes me feel like God a little bit.

I say a prayer of apology for this blasphemous thought, but then point out to God that He is the one who made me this way. And so I say another prayer of apology.

Sin and redemption.

Buried inside me there is an eleven-year-old boy who still loves Katie Cooper and he has something he wants me to do, so I let him be in charge for a while. He takes me to the garage and puts a pair of hedge clippers in my hand. Then he walks me through the Cooper's backyard and into my Aunt Paula's, where the hydrangeas still thrive against all botanical logic.

I am much more careful than I had been the first time I did this, those many years ago. Back then, I had grabbed the flowers by the stem and yanked. This time, I gently bend them over and clip, almost surgically.

Back then, I had tossed them to the ground, piled on top of each other. This time, I gently lay them down in a bouquet.

Back then, I had run away, flowers clutched in fists. This time, I cradle them in my arms and walk.

Back then, I had given them to Katie Cooper. This time, I would do the same.

I hide them among the bushes behind Grandpa and Grandma's garage. I would rise early the next morning and take them to the cemetery.

***

With a fistful of flowers in one hand and a travel mug of coffee in the other, I leave for the cemetery around 6:30 the next morning. Rather than walk along the roadside, I trudge through Bruner's field and enter the graveyard from the east.

Upon arriving, it's immediately evident that my letters to Beatrice Hart and Phyllis Ross seemed to have started something of a trend, as there are a handful of headstones adorned with letters.

Some are stuck on with masking tape. Others have been carefully placed in the plants and bushes surrounding the graves. I see one that has been clipped to the chains on a wind chime. Another has been placed in the open palms of a weeping angel.

And those were just the ones I could see. Perhaps there were others more discretely hidden. Perhaps others that had already been read and removed. What a weird little phenomenon I had unwittingly instigated. And what a weird little sense of joy it brought me.

As I approach Katie's grave, a bird taking flight from a tree branch above startles me. Wings flap mightily and it takes an arched path downward, spreading its feathery arms wide and gliding parallel to both heaven and earth.

It lands atop a headstone about thirty feet away and faces the opposite direction. On the ground in front of it, an envelope sticks out from beneath a small heavy rock.

The bird looks to be a falcon or a hawk of some sort. I stand silent and marvel at its majesty. What a curious flight it had taken.

Then that bird does a remarkable thing. It turns around and it *faces me* from atop its stony perch. The eyes seem human, old and wise. Its white and brown-speckled chest heaves. Our eyes lock for a second, maybe two, and then it expands and flaps its wings mightily and flies away.

In its wake, a single brown feather floats back down and lands on the ground on top of that partially hidden envelope.

Watch for feathers.

Dropping the flowers I had brought for Katie, I walk to the grave and pick up the feather. Then I look for the name on the headstone it had fallen in front of. A simple engraving on a small and simple stone.

James Johnson

1953-1982

***

... First Katie, now Slim Jim. Couldn't Tucker see that nothing good could possibly come from this. He was going to mess up a lot of lives going down this path. Including his own. In fact, it had already started ...

***

James Johnson? Did I know that name? And then I realized ... this was Slim Jim. Something about seeing his real name made me sad. Whatever James Johnson had been in 1953, he was something completely different by 1982. From James Johnson to Slim Jim. From love to hate. From a hopeful beginning to a tragic ending.

Slim Jim was the same as Katie and Ethan in that way.

But who would leave a letter at Slim Jim's grave? He had no family or friends here to read it. Nobody cared about this child killer.

Except maybe for whoever paid for him to be buried here.

I bend down and pull the letter out from under the rock. It is unaddressed and unsealed. Feeling a little guilty for what I am about to do, I look around and make sure that I am still alone in this death field. I see that I am but still feel like I am not. A chill runs through me. Is it Katie or Ethan watching over me here? And have I somehow disappointed them?

I slide the letter out of the unsealed envelope and unfold it to see a single word on a single sheet of paper. A single word that instantly spawns a million questions about the past.

Innocent

Later that night, I sit alone in the kitchen staring down at that one-word letter. I flip it over, turn it upside down, but there is just that one word. I delicately press out the creases, but find no answers in the folds and wrinkles. I hold it above me and let light shine through, but nothing is revealed. It's just one word, but it carries the heaviness of certainty.

Did Charlie write this? It seems unlikely. He had been willing enough to discuss his theories with me at Mustang's even though we hadn't seen each other in years. Why get all 'Deep Throat' all of a sudden?

But if not Charlie, then who? Who else believed that Slim Jim was innocent and why would they wait until now to share this belief? And why in this manner?

Innocent.

That one word was secretive and cryptic. Inked by someone compelled to speak out, yet too frightened to step forward. And understandably so, I suppose. They would have a lot to explain. Probably more than they would be able to. For starters, how could you explain waiting twenty years?

This was a real Pontius Pilate move. Launching this letter into the world and then washing their hands of the matter.

All I know for sure is that after years of thinking that some random hobo had murdered Katie Cooper there are now two people declaring his innocence.

Moose and Charlie had sworn each other to secrecy and assuming they kept that promise, the letter-writing candidates seemed pretty limited. It could have been some random prankster, but that seemed pointless. It could have been someone who—for whatever reason—believed that Slim Jim was innocent. Still the question remained—why now? Perhaps the author of the letter had been afraid to come forward back then. Perhaps the real killer was still alive.

Or perhaps the author himself was the real killer.

When One Child Dies

In my back pocket was the poem I had written for Katie the night before. The thought of giving it to her made my knees wobble, so I promised myself I would do it right before I had to go home so I didn't have to talk to her afterward. We bounced my basketball up to the playground where we first played Around The World and then a couple games of HORSE. Interrupting our third game of HORSE came a call from the street corner.

"Hey there, Sassafras."

The voice belonged to Edie Dales and without even turning around I knew that Son Settles was with him because Son Settles was always with him. Edie and Son were only a couple years older than me, but it seemed like dog years. And being around them was a reminder of all the places where I didn't have hair or muscle. More than that even, they had a way of smiling that made me think I was going to learn a lot about the world in the next two dog years of my life.

Edie and Son were best friends, though by appearance alone you'd never match the two of them together. Whereas Son came with all the accoutrements of a small town redneck kid—John Deere hats, t-shirts that were only sold at rock concerts and flea markets, and blue jeans with circular faded spots on the back pockets from cans of chewing tobacco—Edie always had a country club polish to him. He only wore shirts with collars, many of them with a small alligator or horse or something embroidered on the front. What's more, he never wore blue jeans—always dressy-looking slacks. Somehow, those pants never sullied or stained, even when playing tackle football.

The only thing more perfect than his clothing was his hair, which I never once saw mussed or tussled. That fleshy white crease down the center of his head parted his hair perfectly even, like a Bible opened to

Psalms, giving him a veneer of innocence that he didn't deserve.

It was beyond disturbing how out of place Edie Dales looked in this town. Like seeing a clown anywhere outside of a circus or a children's party, it was equally bone chilling to see Edie Dales anywhere inside of Willow Grove.

Edie's real name was Andrew and that's how you were to address him. Never Andy, never Dales. Behind his back, though, everyone called him Edie. That started one day after Edie had said in a not-so-joking manner that after resting on that first Sunday, God went back to work the next day and made him. And thus was born the nickname Eighth Day Dales. Eighth Day begot E.D. and E.D. begot Edie. Andrew Dales had a grand and fragile ego and did not like being called Edie, which, of course, was precisely why the nickname stuck.

Edie had a ticking time bomb personality. Once, when playing catch with Johnny Swanson, the baseball skipped over the top of Edie's glove and it hit him smack in the mouth, knocking out a front tooth. He calmly dropped his glove and put a hand to his lips which were bleeding and swollen. Edie looked up at Johnny, casually walked over to him, and punched him in the mouth, knocking out a front tooth of Johnny's. Pronouncing them "even," Edie walked back to his spot and picked up the ball and glove.

"Now, don't throw it so damn hard," he told Johnny. "And don't throw it at my face."

Then he threw the ball back over to Johnny who—not knowing what else to do—caught it and threw it back.

Compared to what he'd done to Johnny Swanson, Edie was downright cordial to me, though it was still bullying. For some reason, he'd taken to calling me "Sassafras." Not for anything I had ever said to him, to be sure. These episodes with Edie usually occurred whenever I failed to not be in the same place as he and Son were when they were bored and there was nobody else around to capture their attention. He'd put me in a headlock and toss me to the ground, throwing "Sassafras" at me, perhaps in hopes of getting me angered enough to challenge him. But I was so grateful that he didn't actually beat me that I never really questioned him or his motives. That kind of gratitude can easily be confused with actually liking someone.

***

So here we were again, the two of them bored and me lacking the foresight to not be present and accounted for. I reached behind me and stuffed my poem to Katie deep down into my back pocket.

"I said 'hey', Sassafras," Edie repeated.

"Do you want to go," Katie whispered

"Won't do any good," I whispered back.

Then, turning around to face them, I said, "Hey, Andrew. Hey, Son."

"What say we play a little two-on-two there, Sassafras?"

"Actually, we were about to leave, Andrew."

"Oh, come on now, Sassafras. You weren't going anywhere."

The two of them had been walking toward me as we talked and now stopped just in front of me. Edie put his hands up, wanting me to pass him the ball.

"You guys will kill us," I said. "You're older and bigger. Plus she's a girl."

"Tell you what, Sassafras," Edie said. "You can have Son on your team and I'll take your little girlfriend. Me and her against you and Son. That's fair. You can even have the ball first."

Darkness beamed from the hole that Johnny Swanson's fastball had left in Edie's smile. Like Johnny, I wasn't sure what else to do. There wasn't a way out of this. Edie wanted to play so we were going to play.

"Okay, Andrew," I said. "One game to seven, then Katie's gotta go home."

"We'll see," he said. Then he put his arm around Katie and walked her away from me and Son, saying, "Over here, Pretty Girl. We've gotta figure out our game plan, you and I."

Katie scrunched her shoulders together, avoiding his touch, but Edie just held her tighter. As I watched them, I felt something rise up inside of me and then sink right back down again. There was nothing I could do. Nothing makes a man hate himself more than helplessness. Except maybe cowardice.

Edie passed the ball to Son and told Katie to guard him. "I've got Sassafras."

I wanted the game over quickly. As soon as Son passed me the ball to start the game, I shot and made a jumper from the free-throw line.

"Nice shot, Sassafras. First one's free."

"Make it, take it—right?" I asked with as little Sassafras as possible.

Again Son passed the ball to me. This time I faked the jumper and drove to the basket. Edie jumped at the fake, bellowed something unintelligible from the air, and looked down helplessly as I dribbled past him for a lay-up.

"Two-zip," said Son.

Edie shot him a look. Son shrugged his shoulders and quietly mouthed, "What?"

After Son passed the ball to me for the third consecutive time, Edie got right up on me, guarding me tight from a squat position, one arm on my waist the other out wide to keep me from passing. Eyes on my eyes like a dare. I couldn't dribble where I wanted to with Edie's hand on my waist, but I didn't dare smack it away. I passed the ball to Son who dribbled right by Katie and toward the basket. Edie went over to stop him, leaving me wide open under the basket. Son made a good bounce pass that wasn't quite sharp enough. As I caught it and went up for the lay-up, Edie came back to block the shot and knocked me hard to the ground.

"All ball!" he yelled.

Katie came running over. "Are you okay?" she asked.

"Yeah, fine," I said, standing up slowly, pain shooting up my tailbone.

"That was all ball, Sassafras. You're not crying foul on that, are ya? I barely touched you—it ain't my fault you're so damn skinny."

"Your ball," I said.

Wiping the gravel from my forearms and elbows, I walked up to the top of the key to guard Edie.

"Ballgame," he said. Then he faked left and came back right, lowering his shoulder into my chest and knocking me back on my butt again and dribbling right to the basket for an easy shot.

Back at the top of the key with the ball under his arm, Edie gave me and Son an 'all is right with the world' sort of look and said, "One-two. Ballgame."

Edie and Katie scored the next seven points straight. Well, Edie did anyway. Katie did her best to stay out of his way and to ask me if I was okay after every basket, which began to annoy me. I ended the game with two baskets, zero rebounds, zero assists, two bloody knees, one gravel-scraped elbow, and one deeply bruised tailbone. I was glad it was over.

After scoring the last basket, Edie reached down and pulled me up from the ground. "Nice game, Sassafras. You're actually not too bad. Not too good, but not too bad."

Then he held up his hand for a high-five, which I gave him. Turning to Katie, he said, "Nice game, Pretty Girl."

But when Katie went for the high-five, he grabbed her hand and held on to it tightly. "Nope. You got it wrong, Pretty Girl. High-fives is what two boys do," he said with his grotesquely gapped smile. "This is what a boy and a girl do."

He jerked her in close and kissed her on the mouth, his lips pressed hard against hers, smearing his face across hers. I lunged toward them, but Son grabbed on to the back of my shirt, holding me back. I turned around and looked up at him in anger, expecting to see his dirty devilish face. What I saw instead was helplessness. Cowardice. He shook his head and shrugged his shoulders.

Katie's squeal brought my attention back to her and Edie. Her arms were pinned down to her sides by unworthy hands. Unworthy lips kissed her. When he finally let go, Edie shoved her back and then wiped his smiling face with a sleeve.

"Mmm, I like those wet ones."

Katie spit and scrubbed at her face like it was on fire. Son let go of me and I lunged toward Edie with fist cocked. Edie did not flinch. Didn't so much as blink. His complete lack of fear scared the hell out of me and stopped me in my tracks. There I stood, fist clenched, locked and loaded. My face not six inches from that filthy mouth of his. His lips slowly parted wider and the black hole in his smile widened broadly in front of me. I stared deep into the blackness, saw nothing there. Smelled the stench of his laughter, wanted to vomit.

"Who are you kidding, Sassafras?" Edie whispered. "We both know you ain't gonna hit me."

I felt the muscles in my face twitch and my fingernails dug deep into the palm of tightly fisted fingers. Edie leaned in close and spoke quietly into my left ear.

"Maybe I shouldn't have done that," he said with mocking sincerity, "but let me tell you something, Sassafras. She kissed back. Don't let her tell you otherwise. She definitely kissed back."

I had a reinvigorated hatred for Edie. It came with an intensity that cast a shadow over anything else I might have felt and I could feel myself changing in that very moment. Whatever fear I had of Edie was withering up and dying and I was evolving into something bigger. I felt it happening.

But just then, in the middle of my metamorphosis, Edie pulled back from me. He laughed again and said, "And she knew what she was doing, Pretty Girl did."

He looked up at my fist, smiled broad again, and eased away. "Come on, Son. Let's get the hell out of here."

From behind me, Katie put her hand on my raised right arm and lowered it to my side, though my fist remained clenched. "Come on, Tuck, let's go."

I couldn't look at her.

Walking away, Edie turned around and yelled back at us. "That was nice, Pretty Girl. Real nice. We're gonna have to do that again sometime soon." Then he blew her a kiss and headed down 4th Street.

Humiliated, I took off running and left Katie by herself at the park. A forgotten poem in my back pocket, I streaked right past Slim Jim who was walking toward the playground.

***

"Vicky, hi. Have you seen Katie? She's been gone for hours. It's not like her."

"No, I'm sorry, I haven't seen her. Maybe she's at the Welp's?"

"No, I saw them all drive off somewhere together. I was hoping I could talk to Tucker. Even if he hasn't seen her, maybe he'll have an idea where to look."

"Sure, Betty. Sure, you can ask him. But Tucker's been gone most the afternoon. The kids went shopping in town with their Grandma."

"Can I ask him at least? I've been everywhere, I'm running out of ideas."

"Of course, Betty. Tucker, come here please."

I hadn't yet come up with a story to replace the real one, in which I had been unable to protect either Katie or myself from Edie and Son. I made a slow walk to the door. "Hi, Mrs. Cooper. I was in town with my Grandma all afternoon."

Mom and Mrs. Cooper exchanged glances.

"Tucker, do you know where Katie is?" my mother asked with that *tell the truth and stand up straight while you're doing it* tone of hers.

"She might be at the playground. She likes going on the swings. Have you looked up there?"

"Yes, Tucker. There's nobody up at the playground."

I looked down at my feet and scrubbed my chin thoughtfully. "Hmm."

"Tucker," my mother said. "What is it you're not telling us?"

"Nothing," I said with mustered sincerity.

"Tucker?"

"Well, it's just that …"

"Yes?"

My mother grabbed me hard by the ear and twisted.

"Tucker Merrill Gaines! You stop fiddling around right now and you tell us if you saw Katie with that lowlife."

I came up for air. And the truth. I told them about our encounter that afternoon at the basketball court with Andrew Dales and Son Settles. How I had run away without looking back, leaving her there. I also mentioned how I passed Slim Jim on my way home. And as I told them the story, my right hand wandered to my back pocket where it flicked at the corners of the poem I had written for Katie. A poem that she would never read.

***

I went looking for Katie myself and ran into Charlie down at Moose Thornton's place, sitting on the front steps with Moose, Edie, and Son. Bob and Woody James were there, too—a couple of hyena brothers whose only purpose in life was to laugh at Moose Thornton's jokes. As I approached, they were already laughing in their usual up-to-no-good sort of way.

Hey, look! Here comes Mr. Goody-Two-Shoes!" Moose had probably said.

Yeah, Mr. Goody-Two-Shoes! Good one, Moose!" Bobby and Woody had probably said in back-alley accents like the backup muscle in old tough-guy movies. And then the cackles and howls, laughing openmouthed and staring wide-eyed at each other and competing to see who could laugh the loudest.

"Well hello again, Sassafras," Edie said. He was flicking dried paint chips off the porch steps with a jackknife and didn't bother to look up at me.

I ignored him and turned to Charlie, who smiled at me through cheeks swollen with tobacco. He gave me a truth-or-dare stare as he lifted a can of RC Cola and oozed thick, brown tobacco spit into it, squeezing it through tightly pursed lips. Still, somewhere inside his look I saw a hint of uncertainty. Like he hadn't entirely settled upon becoming this new Charlie, but was trying him on for size.

"Hey." I said.

He spit again into the RC can, looking more like Son Settles than I ever would have believed possible.

"Hey yourself," he tossed back.

"Have you seen Katie?"

Again it was Edie who spoke up, lifting his eyes to look at me this time. "Oh, we seen her, Sassafras. You know that. You were there." Then with a long serpentine lick of his lips, he asked, "Why? She looking for me?"

I turned to Charlie.

"How about you?" It came out like an accusation.

He kept his eyes on me as he spit into the can again and in that moment he seemed miles and years away from me. I felt like I was witnessing a new birth and that my once best friend was fading into the background of this new Charlie.

"It's just that her mom can't find her. I thought maybe you might know where she was."

Charlie smirked and said, "Nope. Sorry, dude. I don't know where your little girlfriend ran off to."

The hyenas laughed. Son and Edie went inside, and Charlie followed.

***

I wish that the visual imprint of Charlie that lasted in memory is of him and his dad bike riding past my house the first day I met him. Or of his giggling face shining above a flashlight inside a tent during one of our backyard sleepovers. But the image that goes with my Charlie memories is the one of him that day on Moose's steps. His menacing face all full of smile and spit.

And nothing at all innocent about him.

***

... he often thought back on that unfortunate day. He hadn't known who would find Katie or when she would be found, but he had known where. He didn't feed their hopes with comments like, Oh, I'm sure she's fine or Of course we'll find her, and this brought him some solace. He just quietly went about searching with everyone else in town that night. He felt as much shame in looking for Katie as anything else he did that day, and realizing this confounded him. Is it better to be a killer with a conscience or without one? Which is more evil?

***

The lights atop Sheriff Buck's black-and-white flashed as he trolled the streets of Willow Grove, a robotic and repetitive message coming from a loudspeaker atop the car.

"Citizens of Willow Grove, Katie Cooper is missing. She's wearing blue jeans and a yellow t-shirt. If you have seen her please contact the Coopers or the Sheriff's Office immediately."

Mom made me stay home while she joined the rest of the town in the search. She said that Katie might come looking for me, and that I should be here if she did. She didn't say it, but I also knew that she was afraid to let me go out again into the night. Into this new kind of dark night for Willow Grove.

Grandma Gaines came over to stay with us while Grandpa joined the searching crowd. As he walked out the door, I thought about that day when Grandpa had chased Slim Jim off of our porch and how strong he had seemed to me then. Tall and imposing enough to scare off the likes of Slim Jim.

"Grandpa," I called. He turned around and wondered a look at me. Furrowed brow, mouth turned down sharply, eyes somewhere else altogether. His nose twitched like some hard-sniffing animal preparing to attack. It was a wolf that I saw in him.

"Grandpa, they're going to find her, right? I mean, you'll find her?"

Everything about the man sank and he suddenly seemed old. Too old for this kind of world. He opened his mouth to say something, but didn't. He tapped the bottom of his flashlight a couple times, flicked it on, and walked out the door. I ran to the window and watched him march out toward the street where he pulled something from his back pocket. He lifted it to his mouth and threw his head back. I knew what it was. I had seen him do this many times before. He put it back in his pocket, pulled down the bill of his cap and headed to the street.

Minutes rolled up into an hour, one hour became two, two became three. And still the streets and sidewalks twinkled like stars in the night sky with flashlights and lanterns. The chorus of calls for Katie echoed from every corner.

***

When one child dies a little bit of all youth dies with them. And a little bit of innocence. And a little bit of hope. And a little bit of faith in mankind. All things pure and good become a little tainted and a little tarnished. There are things inside me once that are gone forever now, replaced by something harder. It started the day Katie Cooper disappeared. That was the day I started to die.

***

When Mom told me how they had found Katie's body by the railroad tracks, I couldn't stop thinking about that first afternoon in the Garden of Eden and how it seemed as far away as Genesis itself.

I pictured Katie's sparkling green eyes and imagined them opened wide and frozen. Empty eyes staring into emptiness. Her soft body contorted across jagged rock.

That was the moment I learned of the depths of sadness. That sadness can make you scream.

"The police are looking for that hobo Jim," Mom told me. "Somebody saw him walking down the railroad tracks with Katie."

***

I never really considered that bad things could happen to me or anyone

I loved. In a strange way, I believed it even less after those bad things did happen.

As a child, I had difficulty dealing with the fact that Katie Cooper once did exist and then did not, and often found myself imagining otherwise. There was comfort to be found in pretending that Katie had never existed at all, that all those wonderful memories never were. With Ethan, the pain came from imagining all the memories we would never have.

They were exactly opposite pains in that way, Katie and Ethan.

Would if I could
Paint you a rainbow.
Would if I could
Hand you a star.
Will if I can
Make it all better.
Will if I can
Whenever we are.

Would if I could
Write you a lifetime.
Would if I could
Hold you right here.
Will if I can
Lift your soul higher
Will if I can
With a prayer and a tear.

We heard stories of Slim Jim in the days that followed his arrest. How he had left his home in Northern Iowa when he was seventeen. How he drifted from town to town through the Midwest—sometimes riding the rails, sometimes hitchhiking. How he took odd jobs, slept under bridges, ate what he could when he could, and never stayed in one place for more than a couple weeks. Sometimes leaving by his volition. Sometimes not. Probably with all his belongings tied up in a red bandana that hung off the end of a long wooden stick, I had imagined.

The theory went that Slim Jim lured Katie into walking with him down the tracks toward Glidden, the next town over. That never sat right with me, though. Katie was too smart to have gone off with Slim Jim like that. I always figured he must have forced her to go with him.

Slim Jim never confessed to the crime, but he couldn't provide an account of his whereabouts either. Before his case ever got to trial, Slim Jim Johnson was found guilty by an informal jury of his incarcerated peers. The sentence was death and it was carried out immediately. Prison justice has zero-tolerance policy for pedophiles.

***

... it always bothered him, how people could judge others without really knowing them or understanding them. Never understanding how a person got to be the way they were. People learn one or two things about you, and they think they know you. They put you in a box that you can never get out of. He often thought about the box people would put him in if they knew everything he'd done ...

***

Rather than sit around and tally up all the unanswered questions I had been collecting, I decided to write a letter back to Mr. Innocent, which was how I had come to think of the man who had authored that letter by Slim Jim's grave. There are a million things I want to ask him. Which questions do I uncork and pour onto the paper?

Who are you? Why did you write this? Why did you wait so long? If Slim Jim didn't kill Katie Cooper, who did? Can we meet in person?

In the end, though, I ended up replying to his one-word letter with a one-word letter of my own—a command and a plea:

Explain

I sign the letter and fold it slowly and perfectly, giving myself a few extra seconds to think about what I am doing. I slide it into a yellow envelope and put it under the rock by Slim Jim's headstone. I consider waiting in hiding to see who picks it up, but in the end decide to wait and see if Mr. Innocent will come forward on his own.

***

Over time, people change and then again they don't. Just like with Charlie, I recognize Edie Dales the instant I walk through the doors at Mustang's. A striped Polo and khakis, his dress is the same as it had been back then. Literally the same it seemed. Both the pants and the shirt were faded and speckled with small holes. When he recognizes me, he smiles that missing-tooth smile that over the years has become a missing-teeth smile.

"Hey there, Thathafrath," he says and I can't help but laugh at the ridiculous lisp.

"Hey, Andrew," I say. And then, remembering how much I hate him, "Maybe you should consider a new pet name for me. Try 'Pecker', it's easier to pronounce and it's stood the test of time—right, Son?"

"Sure has, Pecker," Son says, sliding a beer in front of me.

"Now, thee ... thee, I alwayth knew you wath a thmart mouth. Alwayth knew you badmouthed me behind my back. I wath right, wathn't I, Thathafrath?"

"Yeah, I thuppothe I wath," I said.

"That'th funny, Thathafrath. Yeth, thir. Very funny."

I don't respond.

"Never would have talked to me like that back in the day, though—eh, Thathafrath?"

I ignore the question and sip my beer.

"Bigger and braver now, though. Eh, Thathafrath? All grown up, are ya? Not afraid of getting your ath kicked, huh?"

I attempt to redirect the conversation. "So what are you doing these days, Andrew?"

He slams a full glass of beer, burps loudly and says, "Dentitht." slapping his knee. "No, no, wait, no, I'm a Thpeech Therapist," he says and again howls at his own joke.

It's the kind of laugh you aren't supposed to laugh along with.

"Hey, what'th the matter, Thathafrath? You don't think I'm funny? Hey, you gotta laugh, right?"

I think about that day on the basketball court, me fisted up and wanting to punch Edie in the nose and him not the least bit afraid. Seeing the fear in me and knowing that I wasn't going to hit him. Of everything that happened on the basketball court that day—the elbows, the shoves, the taunting, his filthy mouth on Katie—the thing that bothered me the most was his utter confidence that I wouldn't dare hit him. Even after all that he had said and done. How he had hissed, *Who are you kidding, Sassafras? We both know you ain't gonna hit me.*

"Yeah, that's right. Gotta laugh," I say. And then after a second, "Hey, you know what I always thought was funny? That nickname we had for you back in the day—Edie. You remember that? Edie? Like the girls name."

Edie nods vigorously and gulps down another beer.

"Yeah, that wath funny, alright. Only did hear it the one time mythelf, though. Remember that, Thathafrath? Remember what I did to Timmy Carmichael when he called me that?"

Two black eyes and one broken nose. Yes, I remembered.

"Man, I could be a real hard ath back then, couldn't I? Mak'th me feel a little guilty when I thee Timmy thee'th days, walking around town with hith kids. He'th got two little girlth, you know that? Yeah, probably better off with girlth, guy like that. Know what I mean? Got two boyth my own thelf, but thome men aren't meant to have thons, now are they? You gotta boy, Thathafrath?"

For the first time since we'd started talking, Son interjects.

"Hey Andrew, didn't you tell me to cut you off at 11," Son says, pointing at the clock on the wall behind him. "Maybe you'd better get going."

Edie ignores Son and repeats his question to me. "Well? You gotta boy, Thathafrath?"

Edie slaps his knee and shouts, "You don't, do you? Thee? I knew it! No offenth, Thathafrath, but you're like Timmy in that way. Better off with girlth?"

"Andrew," says Son from behind the bar.

"It'th kinda like … what do they call that? Thurvival of the fittetht—thomethin' like that? You know what I'm talkin' about? That thing where the thtrong live and the weak die."

A fury bubbles in my chest and I say, "Careful, Edie."

"What?" he asks, raising his arms in innocence. "What did I thay? I'm just thaying that the weak die. Hell, that ain't nothin' new. That'th Darwin. The weak die, Thathafrath. The weak die."

I jump from my bar stool and throw my beer mug against the wall. "Edie, if you don't shut the hell up I'm going to knock out that last jagged tooth you got hanging from that shithole mouth of yours."

Edie slowly rises from his bar stool and smiles that missing-teeth smile.

"You gotta blow off thome thteam, Thathafrath? Bring it on, I'd be happy to help."

"That's enough," says Son. "Sit down, both of ya."

But it's too late. I lunge toward Edie and hold my fist up in the same way I had that day on the basketball court. And like that day on the court, Edie stands unflinching and fearless.

"Who are you kidding, Thathafrath? We both know you ain't gonna hit me."

Except that this time I do hit him. And just like I promised, I knock out the last tooth in his smile.

Well, sorta.

In the million or so times I had fantasized about hitting Edie, he always falls to the floor hard, shakes his head a couple times, and then slides his jaw back and forth with one hand. He stands up slowly and walks away with a newfound respect for me. Perhaps even fear.

In reality, when I punch Edie's mouth I knock his head hard to the right and mess up his hair a little, but that's about it. He doesn't fall and he doesn't check for a broken jaw. Instead, he turns his head back toward me slowly, smiles a bloody smile and then yanks out the tooth I had managed to loosen. He examines it, shruggs, stuffs it in the front pocket of my shirt.

"Thouvenir."

Then he hits me with a quick one-two that drops me to the floor.

As Son walks him out the door, I can hear Edie laughing and spewing out a string of lispy insults.

Later that night as I lie in bed drunk and defeated, I whisper, "Mithter Innothent," and laugh at the unfunny thought, at the real possibility. Edie was the filthiest soul I had ever known. And though I couldn't be sure he had killed Katie Cooper, I was more than sure of one thing.

He had it in him.

Panda Bears

Our three tables form a perfect triangle, he and she and I. Her reading, unaware of any world outside of her book. Him watching, unaware of any world outside of her. Me watching them both like two panda bears in captivity.

I can see how she is making him love her. It is in the way she sits with one foot on the floor and one crossed over her lap. The way she is slouched over the table with her head propped on hand and elbow. And it is in the way her long sun-touched, brown hair hangs carelessly down the right side of her tilted head, her left hand periodically sweeping it back and then adjusting horn-rimmed glasses. She is captivating, this young woman.

He practices the conversation in his head and his lips move involuntarily with each thought. He repeats the same phrase under his breath, changing his tone and the height and angle of his eyebrows with every new effort.

He opens a spiral notebook and begins to write. It is the furious scribble of a man angry with himself and I can only guess that he is cursing his own lack of courage. His head wiggles as he writes—side to side, front to back—the way I imagine Mozart must have looked when possessed by the succubus of new music, only the ink and quill missing.

He does not see her approach.

"Excuse me," she says.

Startled, he literally jumps out of his chair.

"Oh, I'm so sorry," she says with a giggle and a slight touch of his arm. "I didn't mean to scare you. I just, I wanted to see if you had a pen I could borrow."

"A what? A pen?"

Then looking at his hand like it has something stuck to it that he does not quite recognize, he says, "A pen. Sure, take this. This is a pen."

They are sweet and it seems to me that something big is happening that neither of them can fully understand. They do not know what lies ahead of them, these two panda bears. They are about to find love in each other. And in the way an alarm clock reminds you not to sleep, they have reminded me of my own slumbering love. I head back to Grandpa and Grandma's to call my wife.

***

"Tam, I talked to Grandpa and Grandma and they're fine with it."

"Fine with what?"

I switch the phone receiver to my other ear. A sharp pain shoots up my side and it feels like Edie's knuckles are still grinding against my ribs.

"Fine with you and Tory coming here to stay, too. With them. With me."

I inhale deeply and silently exhale all the pain from Edie and everything else. I pull up my shirt to check for bruising, or perhaps a splintered bone sticking out of my skin.

"I feel different here, Tam. In my old home, my old town."

"Away, you mean. You feel better being away."

"Yes, away. But not from you and not from Tory."

A few seconds tick away before she finally responds.

"Okay."

"Okay? You'll come? You'll stay?"

"For a while. I don't know, a week or two maybe. We'll come tomorrow."

"I love you, Tam."

***

In the maples in front of Grandpa and Grandma Gaines' house a brown bushy-tailed squirrel scampers across the telephone wires. I can hear the sound of kids playing baseball off in some distance—or at least what passed for distance in Willow Grove. In some further distance than that, a dog barks.

I rock on the porch swing and wait for Tammy and Tory to arrive. My eyes keep watch of the railroad tracks that my two ladies will soon be rumbling over. Three trains come and go. Each of them blare their horns faintly, then loudly, then faintly again.

Swinging back and forth, I think back to the day we brought baby Tory home from the hospital. We were living in a two-bedroom mobile home that I refused to call a trailer. We were young and happier than I realized—recognizing when I'm happy is something I've never been good at. Then all of a sudden, into our lives comes this tiny little something that I instantly realize has my entire world stashed inside of it. I remember thinking that very thought the day we brought her home from the hospital. We walked inside and I set Tory atop the breakfast bar in her car seat. I looked at her and I thought to myself, *Everything— the whole damn world—right there.*

Tam and I laughed as our baby girl looked back and forth between the two of us from that counter top. Eyes wide-open, she looked wise somehow.

"Well, now what?" I had asked Tammy that day …

"Daddy!" Tory screeches from inside the van.

My eyes had been following them since they crossed the tracks, but my mind was disconnected from the moment and didn't receive the message. Memory-blindness.

"Daddy!" she yells again, running toward me now.

I step down off the porch and bend down to wrap my arms around my little girl. She throws her arms around me and I lift her up for a kiss. She keeps her legs running in mid- air and kicks me below the belt three times. I yelp and fall to my knees in the middle of the yard. Still holding Tory against me, I fall backward and then release her to lie on the ground next to me.

"I missed you SO much, Daddy!"

"I missed you, too, Sweetie," I say in a fake falsetto that makes Tammy and I both laugh.

I close my eyes and breathe deeply. When I open them again, Tammy's upside down face is staring down at me and smiling.

"Well, now what?" she asks.

***

With Grandpa and Grandma more than happy to play babysitter to their great-granddaughter, Tammy and I are able to spend a lot of time together over the next few days. We go out to dinner, to the movies, to coffee shops. We talk. We are beginning to find each other again. Learning each other all over again—some of it old and familiar, some of it new and different.

I find those Betty Cooper-like upturns at the corners of her mouth and those gorgeous gray-green eyes that somehow always seem full of hope. Her sweetness and optimism, which I had feared might die.

Over dinner one night, I told her about the letters I had written to Beatrice Hart and Phyllis Ross and she encouraged me to write more.

"I don't know, Tam. It seems kind of weird, doesn't it?"

"No, I don't think so," she assures me. "Besides, if it makes you feel better, that's all that matters, right?"

"Yeah, I suppose."

"It helps them and it helps you. I think it's wonderful."

"Maybe," I say. "We'll see."

I reposition my fork and knife next to my empty dinner plate several times and then drink the rest of my margarita. Her eyes hang on me as I do. Usually I am pretty good with silence, but if there is something being unspoken in that quiet space, I sometimes have trouble holding my tongue.

"You probably think I'm drinking too much."

I caress the empty glass, stare down into it.

"It makes me feel better. And like you said, that's all that matters, right?"

"Don't do that, Tucker," she warns. "It's not the same thing and you know it."

"Well, it sort of is the same thing."

"It's not healthy. It's destructive."

"I'm not an alcoholic, Tam. I promise. And I'm pretty sure I don't have what it takes to become one."

"You've got alcoholics on both sides of your family. I'm pretty sure you *do* have what it takes. It's in your blood."

"Fine, the genes may be in me, but I'm telling you they're recessive. I redirect the conversation.

"What about you?" I ask. "What have you been doing to feel better?"

Relenting, she leans back in her chair and lets out a deep sigh.

"Actually, I've been going to this support group for parents who have lost children. I met a woman from Werton who lost her daughter to SIDS. We've had lunch a few times, talked on the phone."

"Good, that's good. I'm happy you've found someone who can help."

"Oh, and I ordered these," she says, reaching inside her purse.

She pulls out what looks like a business card and hands it to me. Printed on the front of the card, it says, *This random act of kindness is done in loving memory of our child _____. After the word 'child', Tammy has written Ethan Merrill.*

"Wow, this is great."

"Isn't it? I ordered them from this website the support group recommended."

"So then what—you give a gift or something to someone and put this card in with it?"

"Exactly. You want to use one tonight? We could pay for someone's dinner."

We survey the restaurant. I point out a young mother and her two children who are sitting in the far corner of the restaurant. Her toddler son is crawling around the table while her daughter is waving a picture she has drawn in front of her face.

"I think we have our winner," I say.

***

When we get home that night, everyone is in bed and the house is dark. I sneak into Tory's room to give her a kiss goodnight, but she is awake.

"Why aren't you sleeping, little girl?"

She shrugs her shoulders. I sit down on the edge of the bed.

"What's the matter, Sweetie? Is something bothering you?"

Again she shrugs.

"Okay, it's late. You need to get some sleep."

I lean forward and kiss her forehead, pulling the covers up to her chin. As I start to get up, she says, "Daddy?"

"Yes?"

"What do you think Ethan is doing now?"

Moonlight seeps into the room between a gap in the curtains, shining a silvery stripe down Tory's face. She looks back up at the moon, not at me, and I remember that favorite storybook of hers and how we would copy from it as part of her bedtime routine.

"I love you all the way to the moon, Daddy."

"And I love you all the way to the moon and back, Little Nut Brown Hare."

"I don't know, probably playing with some angel friends. Maybe watching us, looking out for his big sister."

"Daddy?"

"Yes?"

Her gaze shifts away from the moon and locks on me.

"Can we go to the cemetery tomorrow and see Ethan?"

"Sure, Sweetie," I say, kissing her again. "You bet we can. Get some sleep now, okay?"

I rise from the bed and walk to the door.

"Daddy?"

"Yes?"

"I wish I could have seen him."

There are lots of things you have to think about when your baby has died. One of the hardest is whether you want his four-year-old sister to see her dead brother. Tammy and I chose to spare Tory that pain. To spare her the image that would be burned into her memory. The kind of image that nightmares were built around. What we didn't realize is that in sparing her the pain, we cost her the only chance she had for a memory.

"Me, too, Sweetie. I'm sorry."

***

The next morning, I take Tory up to the playground to meet my new friend and to swing for a while. But again Swinging Girl is not here. It has been several days since I've seen her and this concerns me a little. It's an irrational fear and I know where it's coming from, of course. Having lost both Katie and Ethan, I realize that I'm destined for a future of irrational fears and over-protectiveness.

Tory and I walk through Bruner's cornfield to the cemetery. She is enthralled when I tell her how Mikey Bruner and I used to hunt arrowheads in this very field. How this land had been full of those ancient relics from a lost time and a displaced peoples. How Mikey and I would roll them around in our hands and make up stories about each jagged little stone. The buffalo brought down by one, the cavalryman pierced by another. The broken points that had undoubtedly been chipped on the bones of its victim—arrows sticking out of chests like tombstones sticking out of the ground.

I think about how I used to go on long walks like this with my own dad. Everything seemed so simple back then, when I was the one looking up and it was someone else looking down. I guess things always seem simpler when you're the one looking up.

Tory loves the fact that we have put her name on the back of Ethan's headstone.

"That's my name there—right, Daddy?"

"That's right."

"What does the part above my name say? I forgot."

"It says 'To live in the hearts we leave behind is not to die.'"

"Ethan lives in our hearts—right, Daddy?"

"That's right, Sweetie."

"So it's kind of like he's alive—right, Daddy? Because he's alive in our hearts."

"Yes, Sweetie. He sure is."

"But, Daddy? What if we die and our hearts die? Then Ethan won't be alive anymore either—right, Daddy?"

"No, he'll still be alive and so will we. We'll find different hearts to live in."

"Whose hearts?"

"Our family and friends."

Before leaving the Willow Grove cemetery that morning, I walk Tory past Katie's gravesite. We don't stop, though, and I don't say anything to Tory about Katie. But it still feels like an introduction of sorts.

The last thing I do before leaving is to check and see if the letter I had left by Slim Jim's grave was still there. It isn't.

Things Lost, Things Found

The Willow Grove United Methodist Church has always praised God with a stoic reverence and I think that's what had me wanting to go to church again. To silence the noise in my head.

This Sunday is special. It is Mother's Day and my wife and daughter and mother are all here with me. Tory sits between Mom and Larry the same way I used to sit between Grandma and Grandpa Mueller. Mom has one arm draped across Tory's shoulder, gently rubbing her grand-daughter's arm. Every few seconds Tory looks up at her and shows her the picture she is drawing on the back of the Sunday bulletin. Mom smiles proudly and squeezes her in close.

"Do you like it, Victoria?" Tory says to her namesake.

"It's beautiful, Victoria," her namesake says back to her.

Naming Tory after her did not make Mom love her granddaughter anymore than she would have otherwise, but I'm pretty sure it helped her love herself more. And the relationship between them was more special because of it.

Mom and Larry live in Glidden now, but still come to Willow Grove for church. Even though Glidden is only ten minutes away I hadn't gone to visit them yet, and I know that Mom is probably hurt by this. She wants me to need her more. She had hugged me when we arrived that morning, but then turned her attention away from me and toward Tory. Swooping her up in her arms and giving her all the love and comfort that had been building up inside.

Tory returns to our pew after the children's message and I get up to take her down to the nursery. Tammy gently pushes me back in my seat and whispers, "I have to use the lady's room."

She is teary-eyed and I know that she is remembering Ethan's funeral and can probably see his little casket as clearly as I can.

Tammy and Tory leave and I lean forward to focus to the sermon, elbows on knees, head in hands. As Pastor Judy begins, I look at Mom seated next to me and I think how she must be missing her own mother this day.

I close my eyes and fade back to Sundays passed when Grandma Mueller would give me a piece of gum or candy from her purse once the sermon started. I called it her "Let's Make a Deal" purse because it contained anything that Monty Hall could ever think to ask for. Monty could ask for a hairpin, tweezers, a hard-boiled egg, whatever, Grandma would surely have it in her "Let's Make a Deal" purse.

Back then I would lean forward just like this Grandma would walk my back with her fingers. She'd rub gently or scratch little messages onto me.

Love you.

My boy.

Hi T (she always called me T.)

And then … I felt it.

Hi T.

I actually *felt it* scratched into my back.

I let out a gasp and jerk upright like you do when stirred from those pre-sleep dreams. I swing my arms wide for balance, accidentally hitting my mom with one arm and the back of the pew with the other. The eyes of the congregation turn to me. Pastor Judy stumbles momentarily, but presses on and things continue as normal.

"Are you okay," Mom whispers.

An instant sweat pours from me. I turn and see that the pew behind me is empty.

"I'm fine. Did you … did you scratch my back?" I ask.

"No, I didn't touch you."

Hi, T—that was the message scratched onto my back. *Hi, T* like Grandma Mueller used to scratch-write onto my back. I try to determine whether I had actually felt it or if it had merely been a powerful daydream.

From behind me comes a muffled giggle. Tory had snuck back up-stairs and is hiding on the floor in the pew behind mine.

"Tory, did you do that?"

"Yes," she giggles.

But she couldn't even read yet, so she couldn't possibly have done this.

"How? Why did you write 'Hi, T'?"

"I didn't, Daddy. I was drawing a picture."

Some people get a burning bush, I get pillow feathers and back-scratched messages. That I believe these things were signs—did it make me a man of greater or lesser faith? If there is a God, He certainly has a sense of humor.

"Daddy, I don't want to be downstairs. I want to stay here with you."

Just then Tammy returns looking for Tory, giving her that hands-on-the-hip mom-frown when she sees her with me. I pull Tory close to me and kiss the top of her head. And when I do, I smell that odor of laundry detergent and cigarettes that I've always associated with Grandma Mueller. It comes and goes like a pin-prick, but I have no doubt. It was definitely her smell.

I want to believe there is life beyond this one and that maybe it exists within some other world interwoven with our own. That the inhabitants of this 'Other World' have simply passed through a one-way door that takes them out of the world we know, but they were are somehow still around, wanting to reach out to us. To scratch their way through the dimensional doors between us. And that sometimes with enough strug-gle on their end and enough need on our end they were able to break through—even if just to drop a feather at our feet or scratch a message on our back. Anything that might stir us and get us to move from where we are to where we are supposed to be.

Is this where I'm supposed to be?

Did I really believe what Mr. Innocent was telling me?

Charlie seemed pretty damn sure that Slim Jim had been innocent of Katie's murder and that notion stirred a hibernating-bear of a thought from deep within me. Poked at it with a stick until it woke up and growled at me.

Maybe I was contriving a mystery so I could have something different to think about other than Ethan? And even if there was some truth to it, what good could come of it now? Who could be helped by my trudging around in the past like this? Not the Coopers. Their daughter was dead and they had made whatever peace they could make with that fact years ago. They knew who had killed Katie. There was no unsolved mystery here, so why create one?

I had come back to Willow Grove to find peace with my own child's death. To learn how to let go. But instead I was reaching back to grab hold of something that everyone had let go of years ago. And it felt good to think I could help someone—even if it was a dead someone. I needed something to fix, but the question remained ... was anything even broken?

***

Later on that Mother's Day morning, Tory and Grandma Gaines sit together on the front porch swing. Tammy cautions Tory to slow down and to stop leaning so hard on her great-grandma.

"Oh, that's okay," Grandma says. "I'm old, but I'm tough."

"When I asked Daddy how old Great-Grandpa was, he said that Great-Grandpa is so old that when he was a little boy he ate whole loaves of bread and rode a bike with square tires. Did you have a bike with square tires when you were a little girl, Grandma?"

"Hey, you weren't supposed to tell anybody I said that!"

Grandma laughs and tells Tory a few tall-tales of her own before taking my two ladies into the house to finish preparing lunch. Old family ghosts keep that empty swing moving and the chains clanking and I sit down next to them for a couple minutes before going inside to visit with Aunt Paula and my dad.

Dad was already in the easy chair watching a baseball game—the remote in his right hand and aimed at the TV, poised to raise the volume at a moment's notice. Paula was sitting at the dining room table in the adjacent room, staring down at the Sunday paper through bifocals.

"Who's winning?" I ask, sitting down on the chair next to Dad.

"Hi, Tuck," he says. "Not the Cubs."

There is a tension to our relationship that had not been there when we were both younger. When, perhaps, the role of father and son is more clearly defined. I think it started when Tory was born and he became a grandpa. The week after her birth, Dad bought—for the second time in his life—a 1967 Oldsmobile 442. The first 1967 Olds 442 he had bought, appropriately enough, in 1967. But I came along in '68 and he ended up trading in his muscle car for something more family appropriate. If *this* 442 doesn't help him recapture some youth and glory, I'm going to recommend a 1980 DeLorean, some plutonium, and a flux capacitor.

When lunch is over, Tammy tells me, Dad, and Grandpa that the least we could do was to do the dishes considering the mothers had spent all morning making their own Mother's Day meal. I start to argue, pointing out that I had offered to make hot dogs or mac and cheese, but Grandpa interrupts.

"The least we can do, huh? Well, never let it be said that Hollis Gaines won't do the least he can do."

Then he winks at Dad and me.

"Tucker, Ronald, to the kitchen."

While we cleaned the kitchen, Tammy had gone to the florist to buy flowers for Ethan's gravesite. When she returns, her eyes are red and she has mascara streaks down her face. She motions for me to come outside and I join her on the porch.

She starts speaking the second I close the door behind me and it's as if I have joined her in the middle of a story she has already begun.

"So as I was leaving the flower shop, the lady behind the counter calls out to me. She held up a single rose and said 'Here, this is for you. Happy Mother's Day.' And as soon as she said it, I knew it was from Ethan. I mean, I *knew it*. I *felt it* and the thought of him popped into my head on its own, you know? Like out of nowhere I had this intuitive certainty that it was from Ethan before I even had a conscious thought. Does that make any sense at all?"

"Yeah."

She sniffs and dabs at her nose with a rolled up sweater sleeve. I reach in my back pocket for a handkerchief that isn't there.

She continues, "Anyway, the florist said 'It matches your outfit so perfectly, I just I had to give it to you."

Then Tammy shows me the flower.

She is wearing a spring sweater that is sort of purplish-red. Like a vibrant mauve, I guess. Whatever the color, the rose she held up was exactly the same. So much so that the rose seems to sink inside of her as she holds it in front of her.

"I have never seen a flower that color before," is all I can manage. I pull her into me and wrap my arms around her, careful not to crush the rose between us.

***

We had dinner that night with Mom and Larry. Since losing Ethan, things had become uncomfortable between my mom, and me and I was not looking forward to seeing her on Mother's Day. Especially since my brother Gavin and sister Heather were both out of town at their respective in-laws. I didn't much feel like telling her I loved her or thanking her for being "The World's Best Grandmamom!" like it read on the card Tory had picked out.

While Tammy and Tory helped Larry in the kitchen, Mom and I chatted about Oprah, the latest movies and books, so on and so on. I knew she'd eventually feel the need to ask me how I was doing, and I knew I would feel the need to keep it inside and grind my teeth to dust.

But she resists the instinct. Instead, she busily knits away on her latest project, looking down through the glasses that rest on the tip of her nose. At times I do not even recognize this grandmother of Tory's, this imposter who looks like my mom, but with smile wrinkles and touches of gray and other burdens of age. She has been a grandmother for four years now, but is still growing into the part. Soon she would be more grandmother than mother, in the same way that I was already more father than son.

It's even worse for her, I suppose, having witnessed all of my metamorphoses—from a baby within her to a man without her. I only picked up the book of her life in the middle, never really knowing how the story started.

One of my hopes of heaven is that I'll somehow be able to re-live Mom's life right alongside her. As a friend, a neighbor, a kid at school—some non-speaking part in all of the scenes of her life. To see her life dreams and her disappointments. I will watch those parts of her life that have been hidden inside of history and outside of memory.

Maybe some kind of grown-up Ethan is watching me now.

We ate a quiet dinner that Mother's Day evening and we had quiet conversations. Mom told us about the neighborhood happenings. Larry played 'got your nose' with Tory. It was exactly what normal used to look like. I kept thinking about Ethan in that heavenly movie theater, watching that movie of me. I wanted him to like that story. And I needed him to find a hero in the protagonist.

***

Tory is lost. Like Katie. Like Ethan. It is impossible to believe this is happening again.

Tammy and I each thought the other was with Tory that afternoon. When we searched the house and couldn't find her, we searched it again. And then the front yard, the back yard, the garage, even the attic that she didn't know existed. She had never disappeared on us like this before.

She was gone.

The thought of my little girl roving the streets alone scares the hell out of me, even these streets of Willow Grove, because they have betrayed me before. Katie Cooper memories scratch at the back of my mind. Like some buried-alive crime victim, they have clawed their way back to the surface and I picture myself having to go across the street and ask Betty Cooper if she's seen my daughter the same way she had once asked me if I had seen hers.

The railroad tracks.

Just breathe, I say to myself as I start in that direction and a Tory memory flashes with every footstep.

The moment of her birth, that instant when Tammy and I became parents and the trajectory of our lives had changed forever.

Slow down. Breathe, I think. Yet I step faster and see Tory in her yellow satin dress at her pre-school's holiday program, singing Still, Still, Still.

Breathe. Breathe. Breathe.

I flash back again and see her tumbling on the sidewalk in front of our house and scraping her knees and hands.

Please breathe.

I keep breathing and breathing and breathing until my head swirls with too much oxygen. I have a feeling of being outside myself. Aware of the panic and the pain and the fear, but not part of it.

The lungs burn and whirr, little machines unable to process the oxygen quickly enough.

The heart thumps too fast and too hard.

And just when I feel as if I am about to forget how to breathe altogether and collapse into sodden murkiness, I spot Old Man Keller and it is as if the very sight of him defibrillates me back to life.

I snap my head straight and the world around me stops spinning.

The Old Man is atop his mower and headed toward me. I wave him to a stop and when he doesn't turn off the Cub Cadet right away, I reach down and do it myself. He looks offended, like I'm the first person other than him to ever touch the ignition key and maybe I am.

"What the hell, Tucker. What's going on?"

"We can't find Tory."

The wave of rage that comes with being forced to say the words out loud almost lifts me off the ground.

"What do you mean—your daughter is missing?"

"Yes. My daughter is missing. Have you seen her?"

Bushy gray eyebrows furrow together and the Old Man looks for something inside his head, and I can see that he finds it. A thought? A memory? A something.

"No," he says with eyes darting back and forth. Then looking up at me, "No, I haven't seen her. Are you sure she's not with your wife or your grandparents?"

"I'm sure. Now listen, if you know something, you need to tell me, Alvin."

It's the first time I have ever said the Old Man's name and it makes a sharp sound coming off my tongue. He even flinches a little like I had stabbed him in the ear with it.

"I haven't seen your daughter, Tucker, I promise." He says it quietly, but he still quivers with fear. Not of me, though. Frightened of that thing behind his eyes that I can't see and he won't share. I want to pluck his eyes out with my thumbs and reveal what hides behind them.

"If you see her, Alvin. Just come tell me, ok?"

***

I find myself walking the dirt path alongside the railroad tracks that I had helped wear into dusty existence so many years ago. I can't stop thinking about that look on Old Man Keller's face, but my mind can't untie that knot.

I near the area where Katie's body had been found and the world around me begins to blur with my quickened pace. The rocks flanking the rails melt into a flowing river of purple and silver quartz. A lone bird whistles and an approaching train kills its song with the blare of its horn.

Stay out of my way, the horn says. *Angry freight train coming through! Won't be stopped!*

I feel the same way.

I am unstoppable with the anger and the fear of a father who has lost a child. I imagine myself standing on the tracks and bringing that rail monster to screeching stillness with nothing but a hard stare and an upright palm.

The blare of the horn grows louder, but I keep moving toward it. Images flash before my eyes like the space between railroad cars.

Katie, Ethan, Tory, Swinging Girl, Old Man Keller, Edie, Son Settles

***

I don't know if it is the wind from that speeding train or the blast of its horn, but when it screams past me it knocks me to the ground. I lay face down in the dirt and listen to the rhythmic *chu-chung chu-chung chu-chung* until it fades away.

Like a boxer rising from the canvas, I push myself up onto my hands and knees and spit blood. I blink the dust and tears out of my eyes, shake my head. Jagged rocks dig into my hands and knees. An especially large one rests directly in front of me. It is one of those shimmering purple quartz that has strayed away from the tracks. With clawing fingers, I dig it out and throw it at the memory of the train and the wake of its echo. The train is gone from sight and sound and the thrown rock lands in quiet oblivion.

That lone bird whistles once more and then all is quiet and still.

I look back down at the ground where the rock had been, and lying there in the divot it had created was a feather. Not white and pristine, but gray and ruffled. Not from a golden swan, but from a common pigeon. Not what you would ask for, but what you were promised. I looked up and yelled, "Feathers aren't enough!"

But when I lift it, when I lift that feather, what I find underneath fills me with grace and shame and hope.

Lying beneath that broken feather that had been under the sparkling rock is a flattened copper coin. A train-squashed penny dated 1981, and imprinted with every memory of that summer and the little girl it had belonged to. Yet another sign to be accepted with faith or dismissed as coincidence. Alongside these railroad tracks where Katie Cooper's lifeless body had once lay. In this place and in this moment. Right here, right now, with hands and knees scraped and scratched. Inside of me is the faith to believe or the rational mind to deny. And despite reason and common sense and all other constraints of logic, I realize that I did believe. In that little divot of earth in this big nowhere place, I feel as if I have found proof of the everywhere of heaven.

It was under a rock and hidden by a feather.

When I stand, it is with a new peace and with the certainty that Tory was safe. It also occurs to me that I am close to that Garden of Eden that Katie had brought me to. I had never gone back after Katie's death. I wanted to, especially those times when I was missing her most. I wanted to go there to just sit and remember her, but I never did. Probably because I was afraid I'd be followed and our secret would be revealed. Or because I feared finding someone else there and the memory violated. But probably mostly because Katie would never go there again, and neither would I.

I walk through the brush and the shrubs and the spindly branches until I come to the clearing that leads to our secret spot. And as I step into that back-in-time place, the first thing I notice is that the pond is nearly dry. Not much more than a muddy pit now, encircled by tall, sickly grass.

The air is stale and thick, filled with the competing odors of decomposing vegetation, worms, and dead fish. This place had once been alive and the air so fresh that it turned your insides rainforest green, made you feel as if you yourself had sprouted from the earth like the trees and the flowers. But everything has putrefied into must and mold. All that had been green is now brown. All that blossomed now withers. All that had been alive is now dead.

Across the pond, though, one big old maple tree still stands. And from one of its branches, the rope we had swung from still sways lazily in the breeze. This tree had cradled us in its arms and it sheltered us from the summer sun as we splashed in the pond. Everything around it has wasted away, but this tree, at least, still thrives in the Garden of Willow Grove. A beacon of hope and obstinacy.

I grip that copper coin tightly in my right hand. There is justice to the dearth of life here.

I put the coin in my pocket and leave, knowing that I will not return to this place again.

Still feeling very much the locomotive, I retrace my steps along the tracks and head back into town, a Johnny Cash song rumbling through my head. I was certain now that Tory was safe and discovered as much when I walked through the front door and saw her in Grandpa's arms.

"Hi, Daddy," she says sheepishly.

"And where have you been, little girl?"

"I found her asleep behind the door in the spare bedroom," Grandpa says.

"Behind the door?"

We had looked under every bed and inside of every closet in every room. We had not looked behind the doors that opened into the rooms.

"I was playing with my dolly, Daddy. That's where she sleeps."

Grandpa spins her around to face me and holds her out in front of him for me to come take her.

"Well, we found you," he says, giving me a smile and a familiar wink.

I kneel down and open my arms to my daughter. Tory throws her arms around my neck and cries out her apologies.

I look up at my wife.

"It's all right," I say, eyes locked on Tammy. "Everything is going to be all right now. I promise."

Tory was safe and she'd probably be forty before Tammy or I would let her escape from our watchful eyes again.

Yet something still feels not right to me.

I had made a pretty rapid descent from my emotional heights and it had disoriented me, but it was more than that. I was still thinking about Old Man Keller and that secret behind his eyes. Guilt poured out of those eyes and dripped down over his face. But what exactly was he guilty of?

Tammy pulls Tory from me and hugs her tightly.

"We thought you were lost, Sweetie," she says and only I knew what she means by "lost." It is a word that with deeper meaning for us now. Katie, Ethan, and Tory had all been lost. Only Tory had been found.

***

... He knew he was innocent, and yet he felt guilty when he found out about Tucker's daughter missing. He always felt complicit when he heard stories like that. Like he was part of some dirty brotherhood and was somehow a little bit responsible for every child's disappearance. Every child's death. Logically he knew it was beyond his control—all of it. Even Katie. Yet the goodness in him brought out that guilt. Jekyll couldn't be blamed for the actions of Hyde, but he was still guilt-ridden.

And now, his very own Hyde—long slumbering—was fully awakened again. It had caught a whiff of something sweet and familiar. Something sugar and spice and he couldn't stop sniffing at it.

The Old Man

A great many things have happened in the blink of eternity's eye that is my lifetime. Space travel, the pet rock, microwave ovens, the birth and death of the VCR, post-it notes. And all of it happened as Alvin Keller sat perched atop his Cub Cadet, rumbling through the streets and yards of Willow Grove, Illinois.

Of course, the Old Man had been a young man for some of those things, but something tells me that the Old Man was probably an old man even when the Old Man was a young man.

Without the growing green grass, Alvin couldn't have eaten, and wouldn't have survived or evolved into the Old Man. He would have slept in a chicken shack and died young without ever having achieved the strange sort of small town celebrity that he had earned because of that Cub Cadet.

No less so than some grazing animal, like some wild goat, Old Man Keller needed grass to survive. But the Old Man had more in common with goats than a grassy subsistence. He had the face of a goat. Wispy white hair on a long chin, narrow eyes that revolved in sockets on the side of his narrow head, next to alert triangular ears. A face shaped by years in the wind, the way a river shapes a canyon.

The Old Man was a simple man living a simple life, and while he did carry himself with a barely detectable air of superiority, it was almost self-deprecating. Aware that he's King of some mountain that nobody cares about.

The Old Man's Cub Cadet growled and grumbled through every summer of my youth. Sometimes loud as guilt, sometimes quiet as shame. Always there, but like the hum in your head, not always noticed. A distant memory vibrates.

Old Man Keller has a more prominent spot in my memories than he deserves and it's all because of that Cub Cadet. All because of grass.

***

From a distance I can see that Swinging Girl is back on her perch, which relieves me. But I also see that she is not alone.

It is not another child with her but rather—of all people—Old Man Keller. He stands next to her as she swings and the sight of them together makes my stomach lurch. He moves behind her and his clingy little wrinkled hands clasp around her hips and I think about that dirty-secret look on his face from the day before.

I am about a block away, but my eyes zoom and lock on the greedy little fingers he has clenched around her waist. As I approach, I can see his beady gray eyes, watch him moisten his dry lips with a thick wet tongue.

He gives her a big push on the swing and when his hands release her, his fingers hang in the air, wriggling slightly as if savoring the residual taste of touching her. They reach out longingly, those touching, tasting fingers.

Suddenly, the Old Man closes his hands into fists that he tucks away into his overall pockets and marches back across the street where his Cub Cadet sits in the Pullman's front yard. He gets on the lawnmower and makes his getaway.

"Hello, Swinging Girl. It's been a while. Where have you been?"

"I do have a life, you know. And there's more to it than just swinging."

As I've done before, I take a seat on the swing farthest from hers. I don't want her thinking it's ok for strangers to get too close.

As she coasts in for a landing, I ask, "Do you know that man you were talking to?"

"Sure I do. He's Lawn Mowing Man."

"Yes, he is. He's the lawn moving man. Alvin Keller is his name."

"Okay."

"What were you two talking about?"

"Nothing."

"Nothing?"

"Not really."

"Well, you must have talked about something."

"Nope."

"Can you tell me what he said? Please?"

She rolls her eyes at me.

"He said, '*You're sure a good swinger.*' I said, '*Thanks.*' He said, '*How about a push, beautiful girl?*' I said, '*Okay.*' And that was it."

Beautiful girl ... where I had I heard that before? Who had said that?

"He called you 'beautiful girl'? Those were the words?"

"Yes."

"He shouldn't have said that. That's not right."

"You don't think I'm beautiful?"

"What? No. I mean, yes, you're beautiful. It's just, old men shouldn't talk like that to little girls."

"Well, my Grandpa is an old man and he tells me I'm beautiful."

"But he's your Grandpa. It's okay for your Grandpa to call you beautiful."

"Mr. Keller is old like my Grandpa."

"But he's not your Grandpa, Sweetie. That's the point. He's not your Grandpa so he shouldn't talk to you that way. It's not right."

"Jeez, he didn't mean anything by it."

Jeez, he didn't mean anything by it ... something else I had heard before.

"Would you like a spot of tea, sir?" Katie offered.

"Why yes, indeed, I would. Thank you, Governor."

She breaks character for a moment and educates me.

"Okay, first of all, I'm a lady so don't call me 'governor.' Instead, refer to me either as "Miss Kate" or 'my lady'. Secondly, when you do say 'governor', you have to say it like the English do. They say 'guvner', like its only two syllables instead of three. Guv. Ner. See what I mean?"

"*Yes, my lady. Guvner.*"

She clapped approvingly. "*Oh, that was quite lovely.*"

"*Too right!*"

It was silly and wonderful to be sipping tea on a summer's day with Miss Kate. Her mom had let us use her China tea set and we set up a table and chairs in Katie's bedroom. The tea was bitter and I felt ridiculous in the top hat and cane that she had pulled from the trunk at the end of her bed, but the company was, well, quite lovely.

"*I must say, that hat does suit you,*" *she said.* "*Very handsome indeed.*"

Blood rushed to my face and brought a sweat with it.

"*I say! Are you blushing? You are! You are! How sweet! You're blushing. Is it because I called you handsome?*"

I said nothing. Just tried to will the red out of my face.

"*Oh, it's okay. I didn't mean to embarrass you. You are handsome though. Truly.*"

"*KATIE! Would you stop it, please!*"

She giggled. "*I'm sorry. I know how you feel. I did the same thing when Mr. Keller told me I was beautiful.*"

"*Whadya mean?*"

"*Yesterday, after he had mowed our lawn my mom had me bring him a glass of lemonade and when I gave it to him he said 'thanks, beautiful girl'.*" *She tossed her hair back and raised her chin to the stars as she said it.* "*I blushed the same way you just did and he laughed at me.*"

"*Well that's gross.*"

"*It most certainly is not!*"

"*He's an old man. That's why we call him Old Man Keller. And old men shouldn't be calling little girls beautiful unless it's their granddaughter or something.*"

"*Jeez, he didn't mean anything by it.*"

I leave my new friend on her swing and walk to the cemetery. I have things to ponder and I do my best pondering while walking. So I trek out there slowly so my suspicions of the Old Man can marinate a little longer.

"Jeez, he didn't mean anything by it."

Two little girls had said that to me in my life. One of them ended up dead. Charlie Skinner believed it was someone other than Slim Jim who had killed Katie Cooper.

Could it have been Old Man Keller who killed Katie?

How could I possibly find out so many years later? There is only one way and that's with the help of the supposed Good Samaritan—Mr. Innocent.

Just like the first time, Mr. Innocent had placed the unaddressed and unsealed white envelope under the rock near James Johnson's headstone. It had been several days since my return letter and I had all but given up on him, but here I was holding a new letter in my hand. Hopefully, there is more than one word this time.

There is.

You asked me how I know Slim Jim was innocent and I can't tell you that, sorry. Maybe I am wrong but I don't think so. I suppose it don't matter much anyhow, been to long a time. Probably should not even said nothing been so long. Still innocent is innocent and guilty is guilty.

He sounded like a man who was done talking, which pissed me off. In clearing his own conscience, he had weighted mine down. Except I wasn't going to let him wash his hands of everything quite so easily. I wasn't going to let him sleep. I wasn't going to let him get away with whatever the hell it was he was getting away with. Hell, for all I knew Mr. Innocent himself might be the real killer. He sure talked like a man who was guilty of something.

I suppose it don't matter much anyhow, been too long a time.

Bullshit. Justice always matters. That's how I'll start my next letter. Then I'll tell Mr. Innocent how he has no right to a clear conscience. That he hasn't earned one. Not yet anyway. I will tell him that if he doesn't come forward with everything he knows that he is an accomplice to murder.

In my first letter I had been afraid of being too aggressive and scaring him off. That approach had not worked. This time I would attack. This letter would be loaded with threats and questions that required answers or caused insomnia.

How can you live with yourself?

You're the real killer, aren't you?

I'm going to find you. It's just a matter of time.

Your letters are being scanned for fingerprints.

You better come forward before we find out who you are.

The next morning, I awoke before dawn and once again I march like a foot soldier to the Willow Grove cemetery. I have a book to read and another yellow envelope that I will place under the gray rock that rests near James Johnson's grave. And this time, after delivering my letter, I will lurk.

I will hide in secret for as long as it takes for Mr. Innocent to come out, come out from wherever he is.

***

I settle into a small space between the evergreen bushes and the utility shed. From here I have a distant but clear sightline to the grave of James Johnson. Any car entering the cemetery will pass directly in front of me and over the first couple hours many did.

Turns out there's a lot to be learned in lurking.

Sunnier than sunny, and the Widow Simpson is walking around the cemetery with an umbrella. She is using it as a walking cane, but I ain't buying. I know the dour old crank wants a rainy world. I never used to understand how someone could choose to be so hateful, but I have come to learn. There is a kind of strength that is most easily reached from inside of hate. Makes you feel like you can take on almost anything you might come across.

We always called her the Widow Simpson, even though she'd never been married. Probably never even had a family, we figured. Probably just crawled out of the ground one day and started hating things. Turns out we were wrong. She was here to water flowers at what looked to be her parent's gravesite.

I guess you never stop needing your mom and dad.

A little while after that, I watched Marylyn Jeffries stand before the grave of the little brother she had lost over fifty years ago and I learned that we never forget and that we live on for each other.

I also learned that the phenomenon of the Grave Letters was still going strong. From friend to friend, from brother to sister, from daughter to mother.

From father to son.

As if in a dream, I watch that shiny black Oldsmobile 442 slow to a stop in front of Ethan's grave. For a moment, it looks as if Dad isn't going to get out and I suspect that's probably an internal debate he is having. But then the engine turns off and the driver's side door slowly swings open.

Everything Dad does these days is either done slowly or not done at all. Dad has not treated his body well in his fifty-four years and it caught up to him in recent years. A collapsed lung, a heart attack, another collapsed lung. Still, he claims no regrets. If you ask Dad, he'll tell you that his health issues aren't the result of smoking, drinking, and the other accoutrements of an undisciplined lifestyle, they are partly genetic and partly environmental.

"Sure, I know the smoking probably made things than they wouldn't have been. I'm not a fool. But that's not why I've had the problems I've had, Tuck. It's whatcha call Farmer's Lung. Plus my Grandpa John always had heart problems."

Like the autumn and its changing personality, Dad is sometimes refreshingly brisk, sometimes too cold, sometimes surprising in his warmth. Autumn used to be my favorite season, the cool relief from oppressive summer. But then I realized that autumn lacks something that I desperately need in my life—hope. Autumn offers no hope. Of yesterday it teases, of tomorrow it taunts. Leaving you to sweat in recollection and shiver in foreboding. All of its promises are cold, the autumn.

With the aid of a cane I had never seen him use before, he walks to Ethan's grave and stands in front of the headstone.

I wonder at the man's thoughts.

And then he begins to cry. The tears come and go like a spring shower. After years of seeing the lightning and hearing the thunder, I had finally felt the rain.

He walks back around to the front of the headstone and clears away some leaves and twigs with his cane. Then he reaches inside his jacket pocket and -- to my utter astonishment -- pulls out an envelope. Dad lived in a small town a few miles from Willow Grove and apparently they, too, had gotten word of the Grave Letters phenomenon. He bends down and places it under the statue of the weeping angel that looks over Ethan's grave.

Head bowed, he stands still in front of the headstone for a moment, then coughs hard a couple times and returns to his car.

When he is gone, I walk over and open the letter.

Tucker and Tammy,

They say that everything happens for a reason and I suppose there's probably some truth to that. I'm sure you've been searching for one. I just wanted you to know that if you haven't found it, you are not alone.

With Love

A Friend

The short letter drains me of all energy and I head back for town. I consider taking the Mr. Innocent letter with me, but decide against it. I will gamble that it will either still be there tomorrow or Mr. Innocent will pick it up and write me back.

***

Sometimes I feel like I didn't know my own dad any better than Ethan got to know his. As a young boy, it was my dream to grow up to be like my dad. As a man, I fear that I have done just that. But having children of our own makes it both easier and tougher to love ourselves. Easier when we see the beauty within them, harder when we see our own flaws mirrored back.

Dad's love for me is Old Testament. It's the way he knows and I eventually learned to respect it. And maybe now I can learn to actually accept it.

I have spent too much of my life being ashamed of my dad. He smoked, he drank, and he always laughed too loud for me. He cheated on Mom and caught my shame because of it. But in this one short letter I learned more about my father than I had learned in all the conversations we ever had. I knew my dad was a good man. And I knew that he loved me. Because fathers love their sons.

Life, Death, and the Stillness in Between

Then Grandma got sick.

She had been having abdominal pain for a few days before Aunt Paula and Grandpa were finally able to convince her to go to the hospital. When she finally did go, the doctor decided to keep her overnight for observation. When he was unable to diagnose her symptoms, he had her stay another night. And then another. They performed exploratory surgery and still they found nothing.

It was this nothing that would soon kill her.

After surgery, they checked her into what they called a rehabilitation center for one week of rest and recovery. I had never actually been inside a rehabilitation center, but in my mind I had images of stroke victims learning to talk again or amputees getting used to their new prosthetics.

That was not what this place was.

This was a place they put old people they didn't know what else to do with. This was purgatory. A place for those who were closer to death than to life.

With Grandma away, Grandpa had assumed the breakfast duties. "You know you don't have to do this, Grandpa," I say between bites of bacon one morning.

"What's that?"

"Making these big breakfasts every morning. I usually don't eat breakfast at all."

"Oh, I don't mind. Kind of makes me feel, oh, I don't know— normal, I guess. Having breakfast is normal."

I nod. "The bacon's good."

"Yep. And everything else is either undercooked or overcooked. I ain't had much practice at this in the past, oh, say fifty-five years or so."

I bet fifty-five years looked smaller from his end of it. The frying pan sizzles as Grandpa lays more bacon in it. He keeps his back to me. "Hey, Grandma was telling us the other day how the two of you met."

"Oh, was she now?" he says as he scrapes runny eggs into the garbage. Then he puts more bacon into the frying pan and turns back around to face me. "And what did she say—that I was an old grouch?" He smiles his grandfather smile and I wonder when that had come to him. It's not the kind of look a man is born with.

"No, not at all. She said it was a double-date with John and Marge. It was Marge that thought you were an old grouch. Grandma said she thought you were handsome."

"Well, I suppose they're both right," he says with a wink. Grandpa has his back to me again, paying too much attention to the bacon.

"So, what did you think of her?"

"Oh, she was about the prettiest thing I'd ever laid eyes on." Left hand in his pocket, tongs in his right, he turns the bacon, looking at things I couldn't see. "Never expected a second date, but I asked her anyway. She said yes and we went for a picnic. This time without that chatterbox Marge."

A picnic. I could see the red and white checkered blanket, the woven basket, the sandwiches wrapped in white linen.

"We were in a play together, too. She didn't tell you that, though, did she?"

"No," she didn't. "A play? Like a play play?"

"No, of course she didn't. That was before we ever went out."

"Wow, a play. I never really pictured you as a thespian, Grandpa."

"Well, hell, I wasn't always bald and fat, you know."

"What play was it?"

"You know, I don't remember what the play was. I worked backstage anyway—props and stuff, you know—and your Grandma had a small part. The only thing I really remember about any of that is your grandmother. I was two years older but still couldn't muster the courage to ask her out. But imagine my surprise a year later when my buddy John talks me into going on a double date with him and his gal Marge and that little gal from the community theater shows up."

"Did she remember you?"

"Oh, heck no. And I didn't tell her about it either."

"You didn't tell her that you remembered her from the play?"

"No, siree Bob. Not that night. Not ever."

"You never told her?"

"Nope."

"Why not?"

"I guess maybe after a while of hearing her tell the story of how we met, I didn't want to make it something other than what it was to her. Seemed like destiny the way she told it." He puts two more pieces of bacon on my plate. "I never wanted to be anything other than the man she thought she met for the first that night with John and Marge. Now, how's that bacon?"

***

I was not the man Tammy had married. I stopped being that man when that man lost his son.

The new me took a leave of absence from work so I could stay home and drink because being drunk helped. When sober, my thoughts were scattered, like a thousand numbered index cards spilled on the floor. And me picking them up one by one, trying to find some sense in the million combinations. I'd replay the night at the hospital with Ethan and feel the tears build. What were Tammy and I doing while our little boy was dying inside of her? What kind of mundane bullshit were we discussing as his heart stopped?

Is that what you're wearing?

What should we have for supper?

Wait till I tell you what Dave in accounting did today.

Whatever it was, I hope we weren't laughing. I hope he died in our sleep.

One thought always lead to another and to another and there was no end, but the drinking helped. I drank to suppress it all and then—once numb—drank more to let it ease back out of me. Not all at once as it came when I was sober, but little by little and under my control. A turn of the valve. Drink a little, hurt a little, slow down, drink less, feel it coming, drink more, knock it down, drink more, keep it down, drink more, can't see straight, drink more, vomit, cry, pass out.

I'd get drunk and write poetry. Some of the poetry was ok, a lot of it sucked, all of it helped. The alcohol dulled the pain and allowed me to express it all at the same time. I let the tears flow freely: onto the paper, smearing with the ink and mixing with the words I had written; or into my drink where I could swallow them back into me.

The first poem came after a phone call one night with my old college roommate Chris. He and his wife had a son two weeks prior to our losing Ethan and it was his talking about their baby not sleeping through the night that sparked me. When I hung up the phone, I doused my freshest pain with vodka and let the words flow like water over jagged rock.

Your little boy cries too much.
My little boy makes no sound.
Your little boy sleeps warm in his crib,
Mine lies cold in the ground.

Your little boy woke up today,
My little boy never will.
Your little boy laughs and plays,
My little boy lies still.

Your little boy makes you proud,
And just as proud am I.
Cause while your little boy is learning to walk,

My little boy can fly.
My little boy can fly.

The night before I left for Willow Grove, Tammy found me in Ethan's room.

"Hey," she said softly, arms crossed and leaning against the door frame.

Normally, I checked on her, usually finding her on the phone or crying alone in Ethan's room. Sitting in the rocking chair in the corner and staring at the empty crib. Her arms wrapped around an ungifted Teddy Bear and that giant empty sorrow that I couldn't chase away from her. She embraced it, favored it and would not let me take it away from her, however desperately I tried. However badly I needed to be able to. After a while I stopped trying. It's harder to feel helpless that way.

"Hey."

"How ya doing?"

"I'm fine, Tam."

She looked down at the empty glass next to me.

"How many of those have you had?"

"One fewer than I need," I said. And then added, "So far."

She moved away from me and sat down on the loveseat by the fireplace. I thought about how we had sat there together the night before losing Ethan and I recalled everything from that one night in my previous life. How she was wearing the black turtleneck sweater I had given her for Christmas. How the flicker of the flames were reflected in her eyes. How the light from the fire seemed to settle over her in a soft orange glow. How our four hands caressed her belly.

"Your mom called earlier. She said to tell you she loves you."

I nodded. "You two have a nice talk?"

I grabbed my glass and went to the kitchen before she could answer. She followed. She leaned against the fridge with her arms crossed in front of her and watched me make another vodka tonic.

I turned around and took a long sip. "You want one?"

She shook her head. "Your mom would like to be able to talk to you, too, you know."

"I've got nothing to say to her."

"What does that mean?"

I unscrewed the lid to the vodka and splashed more into my glass, filling it back to the rim. "I didn't mean it that way. I just don't want to talk to anyone about anything. I have nothing to say."

"Well, sometimes it helps to talk."

I laughed. "Oh yeah? Tell me, what does it help, Tam?"

She didn't answer.

"My brother called yesterday," I said. "You know what he asked me?"

She shook her head and I took another drink.

"He asked me how you were doing. Sure, at first it was like, 'How you doing, bro—holding up ok?' in that macho bullshit way. I said I was fine and that was the end of it."

Everything began to swirl around me. I kept trying to refocus on Tammy, but my eyes couldn't catch her.

"Well, he knows that you'll talk when you're ready to," she said. "And he knows how strong you are."

"HA! Is that right? Well, tell me, Tam—how strong am I? Strong enough for this? Strong enough to lose my son—is that how strong I am? Who the hell is that strong?"

"No. You're not that strong, Tucker. I know you're not." She moved toward me, but I pulled back.

"I think I hurt less than you, Tam. I can't imagine hurting more than I do right now and I hurt less than you—the whole world says so."

I drank down the rest of my drink and put the empty glass on the counter next to the near-empty vodka bottle.

"Now, what the hell am I supposed to do with that?"

***

On the way home from visiting Grandma one night, I stop in for a drink at Joe's Place, one of Glidden's oldest drinking establishments. I nestle up to the bar and wait for my vodka tonic like a baby robin waiting for mama to come home with a big juicy night crawler.

Dad took me here once when I was in college. It was the only time the two of us ever went out drinking together. I had sat on this barstool and—for a while anyway—went drink for drink with that father of mine—the war veteran, the womanizer, the life of the party. I wanted to find something of him inside me that night, but all I ended up finding was a stupid college boy who couldn't hold his liquor.

After I vomited in the men's room, Dad said goodbye to his buddies and ushered me out. I was expecting laughter and jokes at my expense, but none came. Maybe because he was ashamed of me. Maybe because he saw I was ashamed of myself.

"Another one?" asked the barkeep, yanking me back to now. "Vodka tonic, right?"

I nod.

This is the problem with not moving far from home—with not leaving parents, grandparents, and history behind. You can't rub your hands on the mahogany bar at Joe's without remembering that part of your father is soaked in to the grains of the wood.

Grandpa Mueller, too. This had been a favorite hangout of his and I can see the face of my mother's father looking back at me from inside the mirror behind the bar.

My world is haunted by all these ghosts. Some of them gone, all of them living. Memories of them all half buried beneath flimsy little tombstones in my mind that mark that which once mattered or—just as often it seemed—that which never mattered at all.

I hope that in some corner of heaven there is a tavern where I will someday reunite with all my family and friends. Where Grandma Gaines is young, Katie Cooper is grown, and Ethan is just whoever Ethan is. Some heavenly Joe's Place where I can sit at the bar with Dad on one side and Grandpa Mueller on the other and we are all young and vibrant and full of life. So that each of us can be that particular sinner we are meant to be. Each of us battles to hold down the evil inside of us, and to hold off the evil around us. Because evil breathes and lives and is as omnipresent as God. You'll find it in your safe places where it stays dormant for days and weeks, months and years. It lives and lurks there, greedily stealing in sin and in silence.

In stillness.

It isn't always so easy to spot, evil. Usually it's buried inside of some sort of *want*. The want of smaller things, bigger things, softer things, harder things, younger things, better things, things we don't have.

Evil is a dragon monster, but not the fire-breathing kind that lives in fairy tales. This dragon monster is a slimy microscopic parasite that burrows, chews, and claws its way deep inside of some *thing*, some *place*, some *one* and attaches itself there. It sets up camp, makes a home, and then it spreads.

You will find it near you and around you. And if you are honest, you'll find it within you. You can hide and be cautious and you can check over your shoulder, but it will find you.

***

… he had felt something change inside him that day Tucker's little girl went missing. Or then again maybe not. Maybe something unchanged inside him. Maybe it was all just monster food. He couldn't embrace his monster, but he could no longer deny it either. It hadn't, as he had hoped, died after that day with Katie. Which meant it would never die. A thought that depressed him. He couldn't defeat the monster, but maybe he could hide from it …

***

"At age five Tucker is very concerned about death. He doesn't want anybody to die."

My mother wrote these words in my baby book over twenty-five years ago and I have not wavered on the matter. I still don't want anybody to die. This probably made me a weak Christian, but I'll take that bird in the hand every time. This life has always been good enough for me.

I suppose that the antidote to this fear of death is a strong faith, but my faith is just one of my ten thousand weaknesses. But in defense of the Weak in Faith everywhere, I have to say that it would be a hell of a lot easier to believe in a God who took the time to actually talk to you once in a while. I don't mean talk to you through feathers or back-scratched messages. I mean talk to you in a sitting down to dinner and discussing our day sort of way.

"How was your day today, Tucker?"

"Good, God. How was your day? Dinner smells wonderful. Filet mignon again!"

Even better would be God the career counselor or God the life coach.

"What should I do with my life, God?"

"Have you thought about missionary work, Tucker? Or perhaps a career in advertising and sports marketing?"

Why not give us tangible proof of heaven? I mean, to get the big pay-off in the end, we'll still need to be good people and follow the Ten Commandments and help old ladies cross the street and all that. But why make us wonder if we're doing it all for naught?

I suppose it has something to do with the importance of the mystery of faith, but I don't want my God to work in mysterious ways. I want my God to work in pragmatic ways, which I think would actually go over pretty well with people.

Within a matter of days and in a non-committal sort of way, death began to settle inside of Grandma. Still I was not really saddened. Death quietly crept into the room on tippy-toes like some exaggerated cartoon monster and I sat back and waited for her to transform, as if I was waiting for a green light to turn red.

Grandma's three day stint in the rehabilitation center became four. Four days became five, five became never-to-leave. Even though I loved her as much as ever—maybe even more after these weeks with her and Grandpa—the thought of her death did not sadden me. I found an almost anxious comfort in the fact that she was going to die. Like it was a return to the natural order of things. She was seventy-seven years old; it would be okay for her to die.

Or maybe Ethan's death had permanently changed me, made me hard. All I knew was that the fact that life actually ends for each of us at some point was a concept I had struggled with my entire life and yet somehow I was almost indifferent to the prospect of losing her.

I loved Grandma very much.

I would miss her dearly.

It was okay if she died.

Still, I visited her every day. She always looked tired but seldom complained. Every time that I was there Dad was either there, too, or had just left or was going to be arriving shortly. Most times I brought Tory with me. She would hold tight to my hand as we walked those grim hallways that lead to Grandma's room.

Old eyes fell on her tenderly. Old hands reached out for her. Old smells enveloped us, seeped inside. In us, they saw their past. In them, I saw my future. The place frightened Tory, but she always wanted to come. Always wanted to see Great Grandma.

One time as we were leaving, Tory said to me, "Dad, how come Great Grandpa isn't in here, too?"

"Well, Great Grandpa isn't sick like Great Grandma is, Sweetie," I said. But I knew what she was asking.

"But Grandpa Ron isn't sick and he's always here with Great Grandma."

"It's very hard for Great Grandpa. He visits a lot, but it's hard for him to see Great Grandma feeling so sick."

The truth was that I had wondered the same thing myself. I hadn't asked him about it, though. Didn't have to, as he was always volunteering excuses.

He felt a cold coming on and thought it best to stay away for a couple days. Dugan Clark was coming over to give an estimate on re-roofing the house. The truck had stalled on him and he had spent all morning working on the engine.

Grandpa visited his wife, but not like a husband. He came and went like a neighbor or a second cousin or a volunteer from the church. Two or three times a week, maybe fifteen minutes at a time.

"It sure is nice of Grandpa Ron to stay with Great-Grandma all the time, isn't it?"

"Yes, Tory, it sure is."

"It's because that's his mommy, right Dad?"

"That's right."

"Dad?"

"Yes, Tory?"

"If you get sick like that someday, I'll stay with you, too. Every day. I promise I will."

When we get back to Willow Grove, I hand Tory off to Tam who sent our little girl to bed for a nap. I head up to the playground in search of more "mouths of babes" type wisdom from my swinging friend. But there would be no such insights on this day.

As I approach the park, I see the limp body of Swinging Girl lying across the arms of Son Settles.

***

Son takes a quick look around, doesn't see anyone. Doesn't see me approaching from behind him. Her body cradled against his, he starts toward the street where his car is still running and the passenger-side door is open. As he scuttles toward the car, his L.A. Dodger baseball hat blows off his head.

"Son!" I shout.

He stops, turns around and faces me.

"Tucker?"

Running toward him now, I say, "What the hell are you doing, Son? Put her down."

"She's not breathing, Tucker! She's not breathing!"

"Put her down," I command. "What did you to her, Son? What the hell did you do?"

"Do to her? Tucker … this is my daughter."

Son Settles a father? It didn't seem possible. And until this moment, I wasn't even a hundred percent convinced Swinging Girl was even a real person.

"Your daughter?"

"Yes! I came to take her home and when I honked, her hands slipped from the chains and she fell off the swing. The fall must have knocked her out, but why is her face turning blue?"

Gum.

"Here, give her here."

Sitting on the ground, I hold her back against my chest, slide my arms under her armpits, and locked my fingers in front of her chest. On the third attempt, a wad of gum comes shooting out of her mouth. She coughs and gasps for air the way I do after my choking dream. It makes me thirsty for air myself and I inhale as much of it as I can.

"Oh, thank God. Thank God," Son repeats, and he is crying.

Son Settles' daughter started breathing again, and he is crying.

I stare at him, count the tear drops on his cheeks as if they are tiny measures of his love.

Swinging Girl leans back against my chest. I inhale deeply again, trying to breathe enough for the both of us.

Just keep breathing, little girl. Keep breathing forever.

"Come here, baby girl," Son says, and Swinging Girl crawls into the arms of her father.

Looking at me over his daughter's shoulder, Son says, "Thank you, Tucker. Thank you."

I stand up and walk over to where that Dodgers cap is lying on the ground. I pick it up, dust it off, and hand it to him.

"You're welcome, Son."

***

That night, I ask Tammy to go up to the tavern with me and she surprises me with a yes. We tuck Tory into bed and leave her in the care of her great grandfather, then walk up town to Mustang's.

Son is back behind the bar and there are a few more patrons than I had come to expect. I seat Tammy at a table by the window and go to the bar to get drinks.

"Hey, Son. Give me a draught and a Malibu and pineapple."

I must have said it quietly because Son cups a hand over his mouth and loudly whispers back at me, "It's okay. It'll be our little secret."

Laughing, I say, "No, the Malibu is for my wife." I motion to the table by the window.

Son takes a peek over at Tammy who waves.

"Well, I'll be darned. Say, where's the dog?"

"What do you mean? What dog?"

"You know, the dog that helps her cross the street and stuff."

"Yeah, yeah. Just get the drinks, huh?"

"Bring'em right over," he says, still laughing at himself.

As I walk away, he calls out to me. "Hey, Tuck—"

"You're welcome, Son."

Son brings the drinks to our table and makes like he is doing it for his old buddy and not just to get a better look at Tammy. He puts the Malibu and pineapple in front of me and acts surprised when I slide it across to Tammy. Quite the charmer, that Son.

"First round's on the house," he says when I hold out the cash for the drinks.

I introduce the two of them and make small talk long enough that I suspect it might get the second round on the house, too.

When he leaves, I tell Tammy some of my Son Settles' stories.

"So I guess you're not enemies anymore, huh?"

"Ah, it sounds worse than it was."

And that was the truth. We'd had our run-ins, sure, but hell, we managed to co-exist in the same small town for ten-plus years. Ninety-nine percent of the time, we were just two guys without much in common who got along fine.

Tammy stares down at the table and smiles.

"What? What's so funny?"

Looking up she says, "Not funny. Nice. This has been nice."

I survey the tavern and its patrons. Dark and smoky, dirty and outdated.

"Yeah, nothing but the best for my baby," I say.

"You know what I mean, it's nice being together like this. It's been nice being here with you."

I reach over and grab her hand.

"Tam, it's nice being anywhere with you."

"Well, I'm glad that you talked me into coming to stay here. It's been good for Tory, too. She was really missing you. She needs her daddy."

"Her daddy needs her. I'm glad you guys came. I didn't really think you would."

"Tell the truth," she says. "Part of you didn't want us to, did you?"

"Oh, I don't know. Maybe that part of me that likes to get drunk and feel sorry for himself."

"It's okay. I've got a part of me that likes to pull the blankets over my head and cry in bed all day."

"Yeah, but you don't, do you? Hell, you couldn't. Not with me around. You had to take care of Tory."

Tammy and I both know I'm selfish. She left it unsaid.

"Has it helped? Being here, I mean," she says.

It's a good question. Saying yes justifies coming here, but is it true? I was still drinking. I didn't miss Ethan any less. Yet the memories of the town. Of my childhood. There were moments in the day where my mind went places without Ethan. The memories of Katie Cooper and Slim Jim gave me something different to be sad about, which I welcomed. Seeing old friends and swapping stories. Seeing familiar places and retracing childhood footsteps.

"Yeah, it's helped some. I'm no less sad, but maybe a little happier—

you know?"

As we sit there and get drunk together, I tell Tammy everything that has happened in the days since I returned to Willow Grove.

I had told her years ago the story of Katie Cooper and Slim Jim, but I had told it with the detached objectivity of a court report. A detective assigned to the case—*just the facts, ma'am*. But this night, I told the story in a voice that cracked and creaked like Grandpa and Grandma's front screen door. I told her all the me-and-Katie stories I could remember—our secret spot, the pennies on the tracks, the flowers I had given her—all of it. I had cared deeply for that little girl. Tammy sits quietly and just listens. I can see that she is learning to love Katie herself—through me.

"And here I thought I was the only girl you had written poetry for."

"Well, I'm not sure that what I've written for either you or Katie could really be classified as poetry. Just a bunch of sappy words I made rhyme."

She gave me a look.

"I mean, it wasn't *just* sappy," I scramble. "My love for you moved me to write you those poems. I'm just saying that nobody is going to confuse me with Shakespeare."

"Right. And your love for Katie moved you to write her that poem, too."

"I suppose. But I was just a kid. You can't call it love."

"Yes, you can. I can."

I reach across the table and grab her hand. "I'm sorry. That bothers you, doesn't it?"

She squeezes back.

"Maybe a little. Mostly I just think it's sweet. You've always been sweet."

I smile.

"And Katie sounds like a very special little girl," she adds. "I can't even imagine what losing her must have felt like to you at that age."

I start to respond, then something inside stops me. I was going to tell her how sad it had made me—sad for Katie, sad for her parents, sad for myself, but I realized that it was even more than that. Maybe for the first time, I was understanding the impact that Katie's death had on me. My eyes search the table between me and Tammy, seeking and finding more emptiness there.

"When Katie Cooper moved to town … I don't know if what I felt was love or not. But if it wasn't, then it was a sneak preview into what love is. And maybe just knowing that life offers something like love is even more powerful than the love itself. Katie brought some kind of beautiful awareness to me when she came into my life. And when she left … *how* she left … well, I had another kind of awareness."

I looked up at her.

"Tam, the world as I knew it … it died. You know?"

She nods, an offering of tears rolls down her cheeks.

"That's how it is with Ethan, isn't it? Nobody ever met him or even saw him. All he ever was to this world was a possibility. But he was our son, Tucker, and we know he was real. Right, Tucker? He *is* real?"

I hand her a cocktail napkin and she dabs at her tears.

"Yeah, Tam, he's real."

"People know what it's like to love a child and they can imagine the possibility of losing one. But they don't really feel it. They can't, because feelings aren't feelings until you feel them."

***

When Tammy returns from freshening up in the ladies room, I tell her more details about my exchange of letters with Mr. Innocent and my plan to go to the cemetery that next morning and stake him out, which concerns her.

"I don't know. Are you sure that's wise?"

"What do you mean?"

"Well, let's say you do catch this guy and let's say it turns out he did kill Katie. You really want to be alone at the cemetery with a murderer?"

"Oh, that doesn't seem likely, does it? Anyway, he'd probably deny everything. I mean, you think he's going to confess to murder because I catch him picking an envelope up off the ground at the cemetery?"

"I don't know, Tucker. It just doesn't seem too safe."

"Tell you what, I'll bring my cell phone and I'll tell him that I called Sheriff Buck when I saw him pick up the letter. Okay?"

"How 'bout you actually do call Sheriff Buck."

"Fine."

We clink our glasses together.

Then from behind me comes a familiar lisping taunt.

"Hey there, Thathafrath."

Edie Dales stands at the front door, a big gummy smile on his face.

"I thure hope you're in a better mood tonight."

I don't respond. Turn back around to face my wife.

"I take it that's the guy you were telling me about? The one you got in a fight with the other night?"

"Well, yeah, that's the guy. But it's a bit generous to refer to what happened between us a fight."

"Let's get out of here, Tucker."

Tammy grabs her purse and puts it over her shoulder.

"I'm going to finish my drink," I say.

"Thay, no hard feelings about the other night. Things jutht got a little outta control, right? Bethides, you threw the firtht punch."

Still not facing him, I take another sip of my drink. Say nothing.

He raises his voice and repeats, "Hey! I thaid no hard feelingth. I'm offering my hand."

I don't respond, and I can hear Edie move across the floor toward me.

"Maybe you're not hearing tho good tonight, Thathafrath," Edie says, slamming a hand down on my shoulder.

But before he can spin me around to face him, another hand grabs hold of Edie's wrist.

It's Son Settles.

"Let go of him, Andrew. Let it go."

I look over my shoulder at Son. His eyes are tender—not only for me, but for Edie, too. Edie looks at those same eyes and sees weakness. He gives a wheezy, breathy laugh, the fetid stench from his rotten mouth filling the air.

"Go to hell, Thon."

He takes a wild swing at Son with his free hand, but Son blocks the blow and strikes Edie squarely in the nose with a right jab that drops Edie to the floor. Out cold.

Son looks over at me and gives a cowboy tip of his Dodger cap. I finish my drink and headed to the door with Tammy, stepping over Edie on our way.

***

The next day, Tammy and Tory go to Glidden to visit Grandma and after that to lunch and a matinee.

With Grandpa in the garage working on his broken down Wheel Horse, I pack a paper sack with potato chips, two bologna sandwiches, two bottles of water, and a book. I head out for the cemetery, prepared to stay until sundown if necessary. Determined to catch Mr. Innocent retrieving my letter. If, that is, my letter is even still there.

It is.

By 10 a.m., I have set up camp again in the bushes. I pull a bottle of water and a sandwich out of my lunch sack. I am two bites in when my first visitor arrives.

Edie Dales.

"Son of a bitch," I whisper through a mouthful of bologna.

He passes right in front of me, arms at his side, hands clenched into fists, which is how Edie has always faced the world.

He walks slowly, heels hitting ground first, toes last like he's wearing cowboy boots, but he is not. His arms don't sway at all when he walks. It's as if the fingers on both hands are wrapped around something heavy, something he has to carry everywhere he goes. Maybe lugging all that invisible weight around makes Edie Dales so angry all the time.

Edie carries his heavy weights around the corner of the utility shed and out of my line of sight. I wait a few seconds then quietly scoot over and peek around the corner. He walks to a headstone in the far corner of the cemetery, stops, and puts his hands in his pockets. Something in the way he stands there with his eyes looking down and all humble-looking tells me that this must be his father's grave. He is saying something, but I can't hear what it is. Whatever the message, he delivers it with a lot of shoulder shrugs and head tilts, like he is apologizing or perhaps confessing.

After a few minutes, Edie pulls his hands out of his pockets, picks up his invisible weights and walks back toward me. He turns the corner into my line of sight again and after a couple of steps, he stops in his tracks and puts his hands in his pockets again.

Edie scans the horizon, takes in a deep breath—almost sniffing, like some animal in the wild picking up the scent of prey. That's when he spots the Grave Letter at the foot of the headstone in front of him.

He glances around the bone yard at the other letters, his eyes snapping sharply from one to the next. Then he locks on the yellow envelope by James Johnson. After a peek over each shoulder, he makes a move toward the letter.

My heart jumps like I'd just felt a tug on my fishing line and watched my bobber go under. I push the bushes away from my face to get a clearer view. As I do, though, Edie stops in his tracks.

I had been too loud.

I freeze, suddenly mindful of my Adam's apple and how loudly I swallow. Intensely aware of the itchy, drippy, sweat that covered my face.

Air makes a wheezy sound as it passes through my nostrils so I open my mouth, but I am no quieter.

But then something else, a different noise. It is the rumble of a lawn mower in the distance.

My eyes go to the long grass in the cemetery lawn. Old Man Keller is on his way, which is good and bad news. On the one hand, Edie hasn't caught me. On the other, I haven't caught him either.

Edie looks down at the envelope, pulls his hands out of his pocket and makes his way out of the cemetery. He and Keller nod at each other as they pass.

I'm not sure what to do. Do I wait to see if Edie came back for the letter? That could be hours. I look down at my lunch sack, see my book, and decide to stay for a little while anyway.

Questions race around my mind, bouncing into and off of one another.

Why was Edie writing these letters?

Had he killed Katie himself or did he know who had?

The Old Man and his mower had been noise-polluting the cemetery for about twenty-five minutes when he gets to the area in front of the bushes that are camouflaging me. I look down at my clothes and thank God for thinking to put a green shirt on me today when I hadn't thought to do so myself. I scrunch up small as small as I can get, knees pulled up to chest, arms wrapped around knees.

The Old Man went in and out of view, left to right, right to left, blade on blade.

And then another surprise. This day was full of them.

The Old Man puts the mower in park and swings himself off of it. I lower my head for a better view between the branches, but can't see what he is doing from my seated position. I stand up so I can see better, thankful for the noise of the still-running Cub Cadet.

He walks around to the other side of the mower and bends down out of view. When he is upright again, the Old Man looks directly at the bushes I am hiding behind. He shoots furtive glances to the left and the right, then walks back around and takes his rightful place atop his grass-chopper.

As he sits down something catches my eye. A tiny little corner of something sticking out of the back pocket of the Old Man's denim overalls.

Something yellow.

He pulls away and my eyes lock on the rock in front of James Johnson's headstone. The letter is gone. The Old Man has taken the letter I had written to Mr. Innocent.

Why? He is going to mess this up for me, but I don't know what to do about it. Looking around at the places he has already mowed, I see that all of the other Grave Letters seem to still be in place.

The realization hit me like a Son Settles sucker punch. It's not Edie Dales. It's the Old Man.

Old Man Keller is Mr. Innocent.

I spring out from behind the bushes and run to the grave of James Johnson where Keller is quite startled to see me.

"Jesus Christ, Tucker, you scared the ever-living shit out of me," he yells over the top of the mower.

I walk closer to him, holding his gaze. I reach down and turn the key of the Cub Cadet, killing the engine. Its rumble echoes through the cemetery for a moment and then all is quiet. The world is still. Not a bird, not a car, not another human being. Just me and the Old Man.

His voice quivers. "Again, Tuck? What do you want with me this time?"

"Answers," I say. "I want answers. And you're the guy who has them, aren't you, Alvin?"

The Old Man chuckles.

"Answers, huh? I hope the questions are easy," he says, pointing at his head apologetically.

I say nothing, just watch the Old Man squirm in the silence. It isn't an interrogation technique, exactly. I really don't know what to say next.

The quiet gets the best of him.

"Good for holding hats, not much else," he laughs, again pointing at his head. "Ma, she'd always say, she'd say 'Alvin, the day the good Lord was handing out brains, you musta—"

"This isn't about brains, Alvin," I interject. "It's about honesty. You just be honest with me, okay?"

"Sure, Tuck, yeah, of course … of course, I'll be honest with you."

"Good. That's good."

"What's eatin' at ya, Tuck?"

The world smells like freshly cut grass and I breathe in as much as my lungs can hold. One of the fringe benefits to the Old Man's job, that smell. A green smell that rises in rings and swirls from the decapitated blades of grass.

"What's in your back pocket, Alvin?"

"Oh, is that what this is about?" He reaches back and pulls out the envelope. "This letter?"

"Yes, Alvin, that's exactly what this is about."

"Well, sure, I know it's one of them, what are they calling them—Grave Letters? Yeah, they're all over the place out here" he says, lifting his arm and turning in his seat to reveal them to me. "Get in my way when I mow—some of 'em, anyway."

"I've been watching you the whole time, Alvin. You only picked up one letter. And you didn't move it out of the way. You put it in your pocket. Why did you do that, Alvin? Why only the one letter?"

His eyes dart left and right. "Hell, I don't know, I guess –"

I raise a warning finger.

"Don't! Goddammit, don't lie to me, Alvin!" Then, in a quiet voice, I add, "Just don't, all right? You know exactly what that letter is. Now tell me what else you know."

Lips parted slightly, eyes narrow, the Old Man is churning something over in his mind.

"Okay," he says. "Okay, I know what the letter is."

"And?"

"And," he hedges, "I suppose I've written a couple-few myself."

"Why, Alvin? Why did you write them?"

He pulls the cap off his head and runs his fingers through silvery-white bristles.

"I don't know. I guess, well, to be honest"—he looks up at me—"you're kinda the cause behind it?"

"Me? How the hell am I the cause?"

"It was that night up at Mustang's. You and that Skinner kid was talking and I overheard you."

The stop-and-go of the Old Man's confession was getting to me.

"Enough with the twenty questions routine, Alvin. Just spit it out. All of it."

"Fine, fine," he says, the words dipped in disdain. Then his head lowers and his eyes drop down and to the right where he finds the memory of that night at Mustang's.

"Like I say, you and that Skinner kid were at Mustang's and you got to talking about that Cooper girl who got killed back when, what twenty years ago or so? Well, he says something to you about how he seen ol' Slim Jim break into Ben Halpern's house that same night and come out with a gallon of milk or somethin'. Well, that was the first time I'd heard that Halpern story and I get to thinkin' about it myself and I figure that Skinner kid is probably right. That sure don't sound like a man who just killed a little girl. I mean, ol' Slim Jim, he wasn't all there—touched in the head—but he sure as hell had enough sense to know to not stick around if he'd killed a girl. Hell, just look at his past and you can see that. Lots of petty theft and even then he'd leave town and move onto someplace new. That's exactly what he did. You gonna tell me that he knew enough to leave St. Charles Mizzou after stealing a bag of chips but he's gonna hang around Willow Grove after killing a little girl?"

"Okay, so what's all of this got to do with you? I still don't understand why you wrote that letter."

"My conscience, I guess. I started to feeling guilty and my conscience got the best of me. You see, I had a part in gettin' Slim Jim put away."

A million little memory dots swirled through my mind and two of them connected.

"Wait … were you the anonymous tipster?"

The Old Man nods.

"I don't get it. The story was that the anonymous tipster saw Slim Jim taking Katie down the tracks. You're telling me now that you never saw that?"

He shakes his head slowly side to side and with eyes closed says, "I didn't. I didn't see nothin'."

"So you just call up and say that you saw something that you didn't see. Why? And why anonymously? Why not step out and tell Sheriff Buck, nobody would have doubted you."

"That's not exactly how it happened. You see, someone else did see Slim Jim taking that Cooper girl down the tracks." Then crinkling his eyebrows together he adds, "At least, that's what they told me. But I don't know any more."

"Who was it? Who told you they saw them and why didn't they come forth on their own?"

He wrestles hard with something inside himself, grimaces, and shakes his head. He looks at me and I can see that in that moment the Old Man hates everything inside and outside of himself. Hates it all.

"It's complicated, Tucker."

"Alvin."

Unspoken words inflate his cheeks. Then he blurts them out.

"It was that Andrew Dales. He's the one who seen Slim Jim and Katie going down the tracks. Wasn't going to come forward and tell anybody, the little bastard, so I done it."

"Edie? That doesn't make sense, Alvin. Why wouldn't he come forward on his own?"

"Hell, I don't know. He said that Slim Jim used to get him beer and pot sometimes and he knew Slim Jim would tell his folks if he found out it was Andrew who had ratted him out. Protecting himself, I suppose. Said that telling people what he saw would mean getting in trouble himself, so he asks me to do it for him. Says he can't do it because it needs to come from an adult voice to be taken seriously. Anyway, I tell him I'll do it—that's all. Never regretted it either, not really. Not until going to Mustang's the other night and hearing the two of you yapping about it. Should have just minded my own damn business, I guess."

So yet again things are pointing to Edie Dales. But something about the Old Man's story isn't sitting quite right with me. I'm not as willing to believe Edie's story, as Keller seemed to be.

Or maybe it's Keller's story I don't fully believe.

Sacred Sundays

In the Gaines family, Sunday has always been a day reserved for Grand-parents, the gridiron, and God (and in that order if I'm being honest.) And in that regard, this Sunday is the same as every other. The whole family has gathered. Dad and Aunt Paula. Gavin and his wife, Donna. Heather and her husband, Steve, and their twin boys.

Only this Sunday Grandma isn't in the kitchen cooking. Rather she is confined to a bed that faces the window to the front yard so she can watch her great-grandchildren laugh and tumble under a shimmering, but sinking sun. There is nothing more they can do for Grandma at the rehab center, so we have brought her home. This will be the last of a thousand Sundays with Grandma.

Evening pushes in and still Tory and her cousins play outside that window, ignoring both darkness and death. I went outside to check on the kids and to see if Gavin needs a break from babysitting, but he's still going strong, finding it easier to deal with what is happening in the yard than what is happening inside the house.

I look inside through the same window that Grandma is gazing out of, but the view from this side is grim. White blankets over white sheets. Pink gown over gray skin. A nicely framed picture of death.

Aunt Paula closes the drapes, but the light in the window frames Grandma's silhouette. I stay there for a few minutes, staring at the still shadow of my father's mother.

One by one, we each say our goodbyes to Grandma that evening. First her great grandchildren, then her grandchildren. Grandma is too tired to smile, but you can see it in her eyes. Grandpa sits quiet and still in a stuffed chair in the corner of the room—not watching, not listening, not talking.

When it is my turn, I hold Grandma's hand and kiss her one last time.

I tell her that I love her.

"I love you, too," she says back to me. "And, Tucker?"

"Yeah?"

"Go back and look at the barn again, would ya? See if you don't see something on the other side of that hole."

"Okay, Grandma. I will."

"And if you still don't see nothin', keep going back until you do."

I smiled down at her and told her again that I loved her, wanting those to be the last words I ever said to her.

I went to bed that night and waited for her to die. I wrapped myself in the afghan she had made for me years ago when I went away to college and I tried to feel the life she had knit inside of it. It was Tory's napping blanket now and she wouldn't sleep without it, which was more than okay with me.

It smelled like simpler times and it warmed me as it always had. Grandma had made the blanket large enough to cover all 6'4 of me, so that I could cocoon myself from the cold of my freshman year dorm room. She also put a name tag on it because she didn't want anybody stealing it, which was sweet but silly. Guys in dorms might steal your music, your beer, or your girlfriend, but never your afghan. Especially the afghan that your Grandma made for you. But especially the afghan that your Grandma made for you that has your name on it, which was why she did it I suppose.

There are a few loose strands of yarn and one small hole the size of my big toe, but it's still in good condition overall. I wrap it around me and think about how Grandma's fingers touched every square inch of it.

I want to believe that I can feel her. That I can smell her, that I can hear that laugh of hers. And I could, sort of, but not really. Really, all I could do was remember. But when I remembered and I touched that blanket I felt the love and the warmth. So much love, like every hug she'd ever given me. So much warmth that it made me thankful for cold times and cold places.

It would be right for Grandma to die on this night. In this way, in this house. On a Sunday. And later on that night, Grandma did what was right. After the last of us left her that evening, the last of her left us. But when she passed, a light was still on in that window. And forever a light will be on in that window.

***

Gavin, Heather, and I are going through a box of old photos to select some for the collage to be displayed at Grandma's wake.

"Oh, wow." Gavin says muffling a frightened laugh with his free hand.

"What?" I ask.

He holds up a black and white photo of an old woman wearing a black dress, white bonnet and a scowl that would have kept any cornfield free of crows for three generations. She is holding a broom at such an angle as to suggest she has been caught in the middle of sweeping something away, like all things bright and beautiful.

"That's Grandma's Aunt Elsie," I say. "She was a Quaker."

"Does she ... does she have a goatee?" Gavin asks incredulously.

"She sure does. I recall how Grandma had told me how Elsie refused to do anything about her abundance of sideshow facial hair. "According to Grandma, Elsie always said, *The good Lord put it there and the good Lord can take it away if that's what he wants.*

"If that was the Quaker in her speaking, it's no wonder the modern world has left that religion behind," says Heather.

"I guess nobody ever reminded her that God helps those who help themselves and then handed her a razor," I add.

"That must have been the good Lord's way of ensuring that she never married and reproduced," Heather says. "That's a whole lot of ugly to carry around."

A suppressed laugh chortles from my nose.

"What?" Gavin asks. "What's so funny?"

"Nothing. I was just thinking about Dad."

"How do you mean?"

"For some reason, I imagined Dad having to tell us Aunt Elsie has died."

When he had something serious to discuss, Dad would always affect a solemn sort of tone. He would sit down, lean forward on his knees, clasp his hands loosely together, and look up at you with one eyebrow raised higher than the other.

I struck the Dad pose and act out a never-happened conversation of Dad breaking the news to me about Aunt Elsie.

"Tuck, I've got some bad news," I say in a sober Dad-like tone.

"What is it, Dad? What's going on?"

"Well, Tuck, Aunt Elsie died today."

"Aunt Elsie died? How? What happened?"

"It was the ugly, Tuck. It was the ugly that killed her. Her old body just couldn't take it anymore. It couldn't carry around all that ugly."

Then, with a final big sigh and a shake of the head, "She was just too god-damn-ugly."

After the laughter subsides, Heather passes me another photo.

"Look at this," she says. "I guess Grandpa wasn't always bald."

It was a picture of Grandpa when he looks to be about fourteen or fifteen years old. He is shirtless, shoeless, and smiling in the photograph. His left arm is slung around the neck of a boy holding a rake upright like the old man in American Gothic.

"Who's this with him?" I ask, handing the picture to Gavin. "He looks familiar."

"Let me see," Gavin says, taking the picture. "Oh, I know who this is. It's Old Man Keller."

"Old Man Keller? I didn't know he and Grandpa were friends."

Gavin flips over the picture over.

"Not only friends," he says, pointing to the words written on the back. "*Best buds forever.*"

"Let me see that." I grab the picture back from him.

There it is, written on the back of the photo in faded pencil: *Best buds forever!*

I toss it all around in my head—Katie, Slim Jim, Keller, Grandpa, the anonymous tipster, Mr. Innocent,—trying to write an alternative ending to a story that has already been written. Trying to find understanding where none was to be found.

Old Man Keller hadn't been protecting Edie. He had been protecting Grandpa. His *best bud.*

But that would Grandpa …

My mind does a fast rewind through all of the memories of Grandpa I can process, trying to remember ever feeling afraid of him, but there is no such memory. I've always suspected he probably drinks too much. And then there was his strange distant behavior during Grandma's illness. But there's nothing that could lead me to think he's capable of something so hideous. I have nothing but good memories, which makes me feel guilty and foolish. All of those memories are now tainted. Picking wild raspberries in the forest together. Him teaching me to drive his riding lawnmower. Playing checkers. All of it tainted. The chubby, laughing, gentle old man of my memories was morphing into an evil-eyed, sharp-toothed predator masquerading as protector. A lascivious lurking evil disguised as anything but.

A dragon monster.

I thought back to our late night talk in the kitchen.

"Here's the thing, Tuck. One way or the other, demons will change you. They could change you for the worse or they could change you for the better. You could look at the bad that's happened and try to make some good out of it. Or you could look at it and start thinking that the world owes you something, like you've got some sort of free pass."

What had he been telling me there? Had this been some hint of confession?

"No, Tuck, I've never been able to drown those demons. Joe's death did not change me for the better."

It's strange how easy it is for me to believe something so unbelievable. A something that is so inconsistent with everything I thought I knew, but I can just feel the truth in it. It has been rolled in gritty, sticky certainty and presented to me. Not evidence. Not proof. Something deeper than that.

Certainty.

Grandpa had killed Katie.

Broken parts

"You lied to me, Alvin."

"Lied, Tuck? Lied about what?"

"It wasn't Andrew Dales, was it, Alvin?"

Gloom falls over the Old Man's face like the final curtain. Even through the screen on his front door, I can see there is no more fight in him. He is tired. Tired from a life spent on top of a lawn mower and under the unforgiving sun. Tired from lies.

The Old Man steps outside to join me, the coils on the screen door squealing a long, witchy cackle as it closes behind him. We settle into the two rocking chairs on the Keller's front porch. "Alvin" is painted in red across the top of his seatback and "Myrna" across the back of mine. I'd almost forgotten there was an Old Woman Keller.

We rock in our chairs and they creak in protest. I allow the moments to pass by peacefully, in part because I know that it will be some time before I feel peace again.

The sun is high in the sky and its stare makes me hot. Sweat trickles down my face and I wipe it dry against my shoulder.

"Hot, ain't it?" says the Old Man.

I nod.

"You know I've been riding that same damn mower for more than thirty years now? Think I'll probably stop running before it does. Damn good machine. Oh sure, I've had to make some repairs over the years, but nothing I couldn't handle myself. For the most part, I take care of it—change the oil and the plugs, sharpen the blade—you know."

"Alvin…"

"Yes sir, that machine has done me well over the years. Dependable. Predictable. Just take care of it, replace the broken parts when need be. Yes sir, predictable."

Taking a deep breath, he sits back in his chair and looks off somewhere far to the west. The horn of a train can be heard in the distance. It's making its way toward us. That's the thing about a locomotive—only one way to go, really—straight. Straight forward and fast.

Beads of sweat dot my forehead and nose, drip down the sides of my face. The sun is brighter, hotter.

"Alvin, did my Grandpa have something to do with Katie Cooper's death?"

Refusing to look at me, he says, "People aren't machines, Tuck."

The blare of the train's horn is louder now. It's almost here.

"No, sir. I've yet to meet the man as reliable as that old lawn mower. And you can't just replace the broken parts."

"Tell me what you know, Alvin."

And he does.

***

The day that Katie was killed, Grandpa told Keller that he had been watching Heather while Grandma was shopping with Gavin and me. Grandpa told Keller that he'd been there drinking alone, but ran out of Scotch and went to Glidden for another bottle while Heather was napping. It was when he got back to town that he saw Slim Jim and Katie walking toward the tracks together.

"Your grandfather said that he'd be in some serious trouble if your grandmother or your mother ever caught wind he'd left your sister napping alone in the house like that. Especially for a bottle of whiskey in the middle of the afternoon. That made sense to me. Your sister was what—two, three years old? Anyway, when he found out later that Katie had gone missing, he came to me 'cause he didn't know what else to do. That's when we come up with that anonymous tipster thing. I called Sheriff Buck, told 'em what I seen. He figured out it was me, of course, but promised to keep me out of it. You know the rest."

"Alvin," I say with one eye on the memory, "I remember that day. Heather came with us."

"What do you mean?"

"I mean that she went into town with me, Gavin, and Grandma."

"No," he protests. "Are you sure, Tucker? That was a long time ago, now. Are you sure?"

"I'm sure, Alvin. Unfortunately, I have a pretty clear memory of everything that happened that day."

Grandpa had lied to Keller. Why would he lie unless it was him who had killed Katie? The misty certainty rolled in.

"He did it…"

I say it quietly, but Keller jumps as if I had screamed the words out of me and thrashed him with them.

"Now, you listen to me, Tuck. Your grandfather … he's a good man. Known him a long time. A long, long time."

"Just some broken parts, right, Alvin?"

"Yeah. Broken parts, right. But not that bad, Tuck. Not as bad as you're thinking. Just, you know, he drinks too much sometimes and he gets a little sideways. That's all, see?"

He winces and exhales through his nose. It is the sound of surrender.

Best buds forever.

"Alvin?" I ask, staring back out at the vacant world. "Was it you who paid for Slim Jim to be buried here?"

He sighs and says, "No, Tucker. But I know who did."

"Who? Don't tell me Grandpa did it out of guilt?"

"No, it wasn't your grandfather."

"Well then who the hell was it, Alvin? Who else would have paid for Slim Jim Johnson to be buried back here in the very town where he had killed an eleven year-old girl?"

He sighs again and says, "It was Howard and Betty Cooper paid for it. They heard about Slim Jim's upbringing, how sick in the head he was. They forgave the man and paid for a proper burial."

He pauses, shakes his head.

"Some damn fine Christians, those Coopers. Just some damn fine

Christians."

***

Sometimes the things we discover outside ourselves make us question what is inside ourselves and the realization rumbles through our core like a runaway Union Pacific locomotive.

I am only what Victoria Mueller and Ronald Gaines could combine to produce in a specific moment in time. The same is true of them and their parents. Biologically, the men whose genes comprise me—my father, my father's father, my mother's father—are alcoholics and adulterers. Molesters and murderers. Their blood flows through my veins. A DNA comparison would provide scientific evidence of a similar double helix.

I do not feel those things inside me and yet I know that they are there, the little dragon monsters. Biologically, the potential is there. Maybe that wicked genetic recipe needs to stew in life's failures and disappointments before being ready to serve. Perhaps with time and opportunity I will become the same.

What more lay ahead for me? How much more of me and mine is there to uncover? And what was I to do with what I had already learned?

The Old Man had told me everything he knew. Probably everything that there was left to know. Except, that is, for what could only be found inside my grandfather's mind and memory. That's all there is left to know.

A hundred miles of thoughts swirl through my head in the six-block stroll I take through town. I walk the meandering sideways walk of a child who is going somewhere he doesn't want to go.

If Keller's story is true—and I believed that it was—then the facts pointed to my grandfather having killed Katie. Yet there is no real proof. There is nothing for me to do with all my doubts and fears but throw them at Grandpa and watch him react. But how could I confront him? And yet how could I not?

In the end I decide that I cannot live my life with the not knowing.

The not knowing about my grandfather and of the shared blood that runs through our veins.

I watch my feet move in front me—left, right, left, and imagine them overlapping the childhood steps that I have surely taken on this very pavement years before. Taking the long way home, I stroll down Adams Street past the school and toward the park, hoping to find my swinging sage.

And find her I did.

I stop for a moment and watch the little girl swing back and forth. Chained and unchained. Safe and unsafe. The destiny of sky. The fate of ground.

I felt like I was suddenly living in a world that knows shade, but not sunlight.

"Hi!" she says.

"Hi."

I walk over to my bench and sit.

"Thank you for helping me the other day."

"You're welcome, Miss Settles."

She drags her feet until the swing stops. She climbs off and makes her way toward me. She sits down right next to me on the bench and then leans forward on her knees the same way I have.

"My dad told me that you guys grew up here together."

"Yep, we did."

"Were you two friends?"

"Me and your dad?" I smile down at her. What a special little girl Son Settles had.

"Yeah, sure, of course we were friends. Used to play a lot of baseball and basketball together."

"Yeah, he still likes to play those games."

"Can I ask you something? What's your name?"

"Well, I guess I can tell you since you saved me from choking and everything."

She laughs at herself and then looks up at me with those flowery eyes of hers.

"My name is Mel, short for Melanie. Don't call me Melanie. And I already know that your name is Tucker, so you don't have to tell me."

She reaches down and picks up a handful of pebbles and starts throwing them at the metal slide across from us. Each one makes a loud pinging sound as it hits.

I have love for this little girl. It was love that I hadn't been able to give to Ethan. Mixed with a little leftover love I had for Katie perhaps. The beauty of all youth had grown even more precious to me as the world around grew more ugly.

She purses her lips determinedly with every toss of a pebble. Then she tucks that long brown hair back behind her ears and looks up at me with her slightly freckled face. Like a little porcelain doll whose maker has dotted each freckle with the tip of a fine brush delicately and with great care.

I open my mouth to speak, stop, release the breath I hadn't realized I was holding. Bending down, I pick up a handful of my own pebbles to ping the slide with. We sit there in silence until I have pinged my last pebble against the slide.

"Mel, have you ever had to do something that you really didn't want to do?"

"Uh, hello, I'm a kid. My whole life is about doing things I don't want to do."

"Yeah, I suppose. So, how do you deal with it? I mean, do you ever try getting out of it?"

"Used to. Then I figured out that when there's something that someone is making me do, one way or the other I always end up having to do it. Usually it's best to do it quick."

"Huh. You're a pretty wise little girl, Mel. You know that?"

"Yep."

***

All the colors. I can see them as I approach the cemetery. They were not there before. From a distance it almost looked like confetti. But they are envelopes. Envelopes of different colors and sizes—dozens of them.

I walk above the dead, weaving a path between the headstones and taking it all in. The letters are propped against headstones and sticking out of flower arrangements. Some seem to be growing right up out of the ground, tiny little paper headstones sprouting up from little slots plowed into this sacred soil.

And there are people here, too. Living people, I mean. More than I've ever seen at a cemetery when there isn't a burial service going on.

I see an older couple walking hand in hand as if strolling through a Japanese garden.

A former Sunday School teacher of mine has a basketful of letters and is sneaking around like the Easter Bunny—placing a yellow envelope here and an orange one there.

I watch Lyle Weber leave with a handful of letters and I see Abigail Simpson standing and holding just one, a quivering hand covering her mouth as she reads it. Whoever wrote that letter has love for Abigail Simpson. And Abigail Simpson has love for whomever that letter was about. I never believed in the possibility of either of those things until this moment.

Beatrice Hart sits cross-legged in front of Laura Jane's headstone with several open letters stacked neatly at her side. At least that many more in front of her waiting to be opened and read.

There are five letters at Ethan's gravesite and two at Katie's. There are about to be three.

From my back pocket I pull out the letter I had written for Howard and Betty Cooper before coming out here. The envelope also contains the poem that I had written for Katie those many years ago and a letter to the Coopers explaining the story behind it. I had not set out to write the Coopers a Grave Letter, but after leaving Swinging Girl at the park I had gone back to confront Grandpa only to find the house empty.

I had stood in the living room staring at the picture of Grandpa and Grandma at the altar on the day of their wedding. I stared into the face of my grandfather and he stared right back at me through time. My eyes bounced across the frozen faces of the children and grandchildren and great grandchildren that surrounded them on that wall. The clocks ticked at me. It was when I looked back at Grandpa that the idea came to me. Almost as if it came from that man in that wedding photo. That man on that day. That man that Grandpa had intended on being forever.

I went upstairs to the attic and pulled the poem out from beneath the floor plank where I had hidden it the day of Katie's funeral. There was a part of me that was going to be embarrassed for the Coopers to read that poem that little boy me had written for their daughter. But I knew it would bring them some joy and I could not deprive them of that.

I added my letter to the pile at Katie's grave and left the cemetery.

Silent Killers

Finally, a blip.

And then another.

And another.

But the nurse kept adjusting the fetal heart monitor around my wife's belly.

Tammy saw that I was confused. "That's mine, Tucker," she said. "That's my heartbeat."

The nurse asked us if this was our first child—*no, we have a four year-old girl.*

If we knew what we were having—*yes, a boy.*

If we had a name picked out—*yes, Ethan.*

She loosened the strap, repositioned Tammy in the bed, tightened the strap.

"He's hiding from me, the little stinker. I'm going to get Nurse Graham and ask her to try. I'm always having trouble with these things. I'll be right back."

Tammy turned to me and with her eyes alone she told me something was wrong. Those eyes pleaded for help and they asked for forgiveness. She tried a smile, but the tears came. One hand went over her eyes as if protecting them from some horrid sight. The other hand reached up and then back down again looking for something to hurt or something to hold.

I was leaning against the window, legs getting more and more unsteady with every second I couldn't hear our baby's heartbeat. I moved to her side.

"Tucker, I'm so scared."

"No, Tam. No. Everything's going to be fine. Right? Everything's going to be fine."

150

***

The room was full of white things, silver things, fluorescent things. The door opened and Dr. Connelly stepped in slowly. She had trouble lifting her eyes against the gravity of the situation. She inhaled deep and then spoke.

"Mr. and Mrs. Gaines, you ... know what's happened, don't you?"

And here's what you think about in the moments after you find out that your baby has died ...

You think about that Saturday morning that your wife sent you into the bathroom to read the results of the home pregnancy test that she had purchased and taken without your knowledge. How long ago that day seemed, and longer still the next one like it.

You think about how losing a child feels both the same and different as you had imagined. Like the difference between being alone in a room and alone in the world.

You think about those who will explain that this was God punishing for sin and you hate them for it. And you hate yourself equally for having the same thought.

You think about all the people that should have died before this child and how capable you are of killing them yourself in this moment. Your father. Your mother. You could kill them by your own hand if it would save your baby. If it would set the world right.

You think about the Hendricks, friends of your family who lost their grown son in a farm accident the year before and you are jealous of their memories because you already realize that this one memory, this day of your child's death and birth, was the only one you're ever going to have of him before he was tucked into a coffin, dropped into the earth, and forgotten by a world that cycled without relent. How invaluable memories suddenly seemed to you. And how utterly unattainable.

You think about how much people will care and how much they won't. How much they will understand and how much they won't. How they will try to put this tragedy in a smaller box by comparing it to what they deem to be bigger tragedies.

Stillbirth was not birth. Stillbirth was stillbirth.

And you think about Katie Cooper. How this was how her parents must have felt when she had died.

Was this how you felt, Howard Cooper? Were you some new kind of lost? Were you some new word for sad? Were you something far greater than angry? Far, far greater than the worst, most bitter, vile tasting, spit-spit-spit, hate-hate-hate, don't-look-at-me, curse-the-world, angry you had ever known? Was that what it was for you when your daughter turned up dead, Howard Cooper? Did you have to stand and look on stupidly at a broken wife you couldn't take care of? Did you have to helplessly watch her endure a pain and horror that made your own feel small? Made you ashamed of your own pain until you hated it? Did your hands never feel so empty? Did your hugs never feel so cold? Did you never feel more a failure?

You were sad when Katie Cooper died, very sad. Not as sad as Howard Cooper had been then. Not as sad as you are now.

***

I knew that Mom and Larry would be anxious for news. Not to mention Tory. I didn't want to make that phone call. I didn't want to say the words out loud. I didn't want them to hurt like I knew they would. And for reasons I did not understand, I was humiliated. Like I had been the butt of some cruel joke and would now have to face a laughing world.

I picked up the phone and dialed.

I searched for the right words to use. My head raced in wispy little thought-circles. Falling from a building and grabbing for something that had never been there.

What does stillbirth mean? Was he ever alive? Did he exist? Was it better to not have known him at all? Would memories make it hurt more? Am I supposed to hurt this much? Did he ever exist?

"Hello?" Mom said anxiously.

It took me a second to gather myself.

"Mom ... we lost the baby."

"I'll be right there," she said.

***

Dr. Connelly advised us that the safest way forward was to let Tammy have the baby naturally. Mom and I sat in chairs on either side of Tammy in the bed between us. The three of us sat and waited for contractions, the unrelenting portent of birth and death, alpha and omega. We prayed for a miracle and why not? Why shouldn't there be one? If not for me, for Tammy. At least for my beautiful wife who lay there in that cold dark room feeling like the most horrible of failures. The child who had lost her mother was now a mother who had lost her child.

We prayed and cried through the long night that was not long enough. I was shamefully weak and had neither the strength nor the will to so much as stand upright. I watched my mom spoon-feed Tammy ice chips and dampen her brow with a cold wet rag. She stroked her hair like a mother strokes her sleeping child, pulling the loose strands away from Tammy's face.

Tammy and I would look into each other's eyes and turn away when we could not stand what we saw there. Her eyes searched mine for forgiveness or protection or answers or something else that I could not provide. She knew what lay ahead of her. Knew it could not be avoided. Birth and death.

I was tired with the weariness that comes from seeking and not finding. There was nothing I could do to help either mother or son. I stared at myself in the bathroom mirror several times during that eternal night, looking for something that hadn't been there before, but I didn't look any different. I needed a wound, wanted a scar. Some sort of permanent disfigurement to mark the moment. But there was nothing, I still looked the same. How in God's name could I look the same? I forced a smile just to see if my face was still capable of making one. Just to see if I could see anything behind it or in front of it, but my smile still looked like my smile.

"Your son is dead," I kept saying to myself. "Your son is dead."

After six hours of labor, Ethan arrived early the next morning. The delivery was normal in so many ways. Screams and cries. Blood and tears. Tammy delivering our still baby may have been the greatest act of strength I have ever witnessed. I sat in my chair defeated through much of the delivery. But this woman, this love of mine, this *mother* found the strength to push when it was against her every instinct. I knew her thoughts. *Stay here. Stay with me, inside me. We can pretend it all away. We can pretend everything better and I will never let you go. I am your mommy and I will never let you go.*

We did not get our miracle. Ethan Merrill Gaines came into this world in a haunting silence. Dr. Connelly lifted him to me and let me cut the cord that linked him to his mother. The cord that wrapped around his neck, brought him to death. And in that moment, as I severed that connection, all was calm and peaceful and far too quiet. As if the world had gone still with him.

The surgical scissors clinked when I set them down on the tray. And I began to sob and it killed all that quiet, reawakened the world.

The nurse helped me bathe and dress Ethan and I presented him to his mother. She cradled him in the nook of her arm, looked down at him like a memory. He was still warm and Tammy closed her eyes, held him to her chest and pressed her cheek against his, allowing herself one more moment to pretend.

She then gave him to me and I began holding him forever. I held my son and felt his body steadily cool, despite all my efforts of warmth. His hair was dark and had a curl to it like my own. Tammy told me that he had my nose, which I desperately wanted to see but could not. I did think that he looked like his big sister Tory, though. I parted his eyelids to see eyes of blue and I counted fingers and toes. Blood poured from his nose and I dabbed it away with the corners of the blanket. His jaw was slack and his mouth kept falling open. I gently held it shut, closed my eyes, and held him against me tight. Tried to squeeze him into me. I felt him in my arms and knew that he was real. Knew that he had existed. Ethan Merrill Gaines had lived.

I rocked in the chair, repeating over and over the only words that came to me.

"My poor little boy. My poor little boy."

***

Bloody-knuckled hands are choking the life and breath out of my grand-father. He gasps and I see Ethan suffocating inside of his mother. Umbilical cord around his neck, not understanding what was happening. Not knowing that all he needed was just a little bit of air. Not able to untangle himself from his lifeline. The thought of my dead son softens me briefly and my grip loosens. Grandpa coughs and chokes and sucks in air greedily.

Not moving from my straddling position across his chest, I lift my eyes to the picture that hangs on the wall in front of me. Grandpa and Grandma on their wedding day. Standing there together hand in hand, not knowing what life has in store for them. Unable to foresee this moment some fifty-plus years in the future when the groom would be killed by the son of his son.

The groom smiles at me. What had happened to this man? Where had he gone? I stare hard, looking for some semblance of the creature that is beneath me now. Some hint of the evil that lurks within, but I cannot see the dragon monster. There is no evil in the groom. Life put it there later, to be sure, because there is no evil inside the man in the picture.

I am surrounded by the evidence of the life that followed this picture moment and I search for clues in them. Every wall and table top is covered with the evidence of normalcy. Delicates and figurines, gifts from over the years. Old pictures of things that were once new and new pictures of things that had become old. Ceramic things, knitted things, embroidered things. Souvenir dishes from Niagara Falls, The Alamo, Mt. Rushmore.

On the table by the door is a green kerosene lamp that has gone from modern convenience to useless artifact without itself ever having changed. The lamp is aged and not aged, it is the world around it that has changed.

There is no explanation. At some point, the man in the picture had been killed by the man in my hands. The man in my hands, like some pod creature replacement, has crept in and stole the good man's life. He quietly assumed his role. He steadily hurt and he silently killed. Like whatever evil was responsible for killing Ethan, this pod creature silently killed.

The grandfather clock in the corner dongs. How many times I do not notice, but it feels like it is counting backwards. Suddenly all the walls are covered in clocks. I snap my head around and lock on each one. So much inconsonant ticking and tocking that there is no sound space left for quiet.

No room for stillness or the still.

The clocks grow louder. Behind the sound of their taunts I can hear the faint sound of Grandpa's voice. His hands are clasped around my wrists, attempting to release the grip I have on his neck. The clocks grow louder still and drown him out completely. I look him in the eye and he loosens his hold on my wrists.

I think about Katie and tighten my grip.

I think about Ethan and squeezed until Grandpa's face is purple and bruised looking. Until blood pours from his nose and onto my fingers. Until blood oozes from his ears. Until vomit shoots from mouth. Until eyes pop out of sockets and I find myself staring into empty sockets.

Until all of life has left him.

I'm the silent killer.

That was the thought that was echoing through me when I awake the next morning.

The dream had been so real. The kind of real that has you wondering when you wake up whether it really happened or whether you have been blessed with a nightmare.

I don't get out of bed. I don't mind-check for pain or soreness. I don't even open my eyes.

I do wonder whether my fists are bloody, but I don't dare check.

For a moment, I wonder if maybe it all really did happen. But even if it didn't, I do not question whether I am capable. Because I know now that I am. It is in me. I can do it.

I can kill.

***

... he wasn't a killer. Yes, he had killed, but that didn't make him a killer. It had not been his intent to kill Katie. And he had felt the crushing guilt of what he done every day since. He latched on to that guilt as evidence of his innate goodness. He was a good man who had done a terrible thing. But only a good man could feel bad about doing evil ...

***

Something electric and wiry snakes its way through my brain. Lips dry and tongue thick, I reach blindly to my nightstand for the glass of water that isn't there. I squish my head between both hands to suppress the pain that came from sitting up too quickly. I rub my eyes and remember the night before ...

***

Tammy and Tory packed up their stuff and have left for home. I am alone. The emptiness of this house is haunting and for the first time in my life, I am afraid to be alone here. I make myself a vodka tonic. Then a second and a third. I drink them in silence in the chair that had been Grandma's.

Knitting needles and yarn stick out from the bag beside the chair, an almost finished white and blue baby blanket stuffed down inside of it. On the end table is a TV Guide with an unfunny sitcom star on the cover. A universal remote. A coaster. A rotary phone. A lamp.

A distorted version of me stares back from the black screen of the television.

Around me the walls are covered with photographs of family. The picture of Grandpa and Grandma on their wedding day in the center of one wall, surrounded by everyone who ultimately came from them.

The clocks tick and tock loudly in their offbeat rhythms the same way they did in my dream. In sync with none of it, my heart still beats. Chest rising and falling unnaturally, I force the air out of me. Blood pulsates through my body in quiet fury, causing muscles to throb and fingers to curl.

And then, finally, the sound of something heavy on the steps of the back porch. I count the steps until the screen door squeals open and my grandfather steps inside.

He says hi and I say something back that comes out slurred and unintelligible.

"You're drunk," he says with a smirk and a hint of approval.

"Worse things to be."

I drink from my vodka tonic and slurp up the ice cubes, swirling them around the inside of my mouth before crunching them to water. I set the drink on the table and stare outside through the picture window in front of me. The same window Grandma had stared through as she lay in bed dying.

"Just an observation. Not a judgment."

"Judge not lest ye be judged, right?"

He looks at me sideways, wolfish eyes narrow and probing. I have seen this in him once before. It was the night he went searching for Katie Cooper with the rest of the town.

"Grandpa, they're going to find her, right? I mean, you'll find her?"

"Think I'll make myself a drink, too" he growls. "Seems like a good night to get drunk."

He comes back a couple minutes later with four fingers of Scotch in a tumbler, no ice. He sits down in the chair opposite from me and takes a sip.

With a fiery exhale, he says, "Where are your ladies at? In bed already?"

"Gone. And they won't be coming back."

I stare at him hard, but he holds my gaze. No hints revealed in the eyes of the wolf.

"That's too bad. I liked having them here. Helped fill the emptiness your Grandma left. I suppose that means you'll be going soon, too."

"Why didn't you visit Grandma more in the nursing home?"

I had wanted to ask him why he killed Katie Cooper, but this came out instead.

He leans forward in his chair and hangs his head.

"I know. I know, Tuck. I should have, but I just … I couldn't stand seeing her like that. I know it's not right, but your Grandma understood. Believe me, she understood."

"Understood what, that you put your own feelings ahead of hers as she lay on her deathbed?"

"I suppose you could put it that way. I ain't justifying it, Tuck. I'm telling you I was wrong."

"You knew it was wrong then, but you did it anyway."

"Yes, I suppose I did," he says dismissively.

Blood and alcohol race to my head as I rise from the chair.

"You knew it was wrong then, but you did it anyway," I repeat.

"I heard you the first time," Grandpa says defiantly. "What do you want me to say? I'm sorry, okay?"

"YOU KNEW IT WAS WRONG THEN, BUT YOU DID ANYWAY!" I shout.

And in the heavy quietness that followed, I realize that I am standing above Grandpa now and pointing out the window behind him. Pointing at the Cooper's house.

Fear in those wolf eyes now, they dart around. Then a slight shift of his head as he looks over his shoulder at what I am pointing at. What he already knows is there. He gathers himself and stands.

"I'm getting another drink. Maybe you ought to do the same."

As he tries to slip by me, I grab his shoulder, whip him back around, and shove him down into his chair again.

"NO! No, Grandpa. I'm not finished."

In my rage, I had clipped him on the nose and he is bleeding. He squeezes at it gently, wipes a bare arm across his face and smears the blood.

"What the hell are you doing, Tuck?" he whispers.

"Just trying to figure some things out, Grandpa."

The word hangs on my lips like a dying breath—*Grandpaaah.*

My father's father. His blood in my blood. The weight of it all sunk me and I briefly consider forgiveness because it seems like the best way to be able to love myself. But it's only a moment and in the end I decide that it is my fate to love us both less.

"Grandpa," I repeat, checking the taste of the word on my tongue.

All tenderness has been drained from the word and in its place all things wicked. All things unnatural. All things heinous.

"Why did you tell Alvin Keller that you saw James Johnson with Katie Cooper the day that she was killed?"

"What? James who?"

"Johnson. That was Slim Jim's real name. James Johnson. Now, why did you tell Old Man Keller you saw him with Katie?"

"How the hell—who told you about that? Alvin tell you that?"

"Never mind how I found out, just answer the damn question. Why did you say you saw them together?"

"Because I did."

"No. You didn't."

"Yeah, I did, Tuck. I seen them as I was coming back in from town. I had run out to buy some whiskey," he says lifting his glass of Scotch as evidence of the claim. "I know I shouldn't have left your sister like that, but I did. And I seen them when I come back into town."

I tell him about Slim Jim's late night snack at the Halperns that very night.

"Does that sound like the actions of a man who's just killed a little girl?"

"How the hell should I know? That Slim Jim was nutty as a fruitcake, everyone knew that."

He gets up again and pushes his way past me, the blood on his arm smears across my shirt.

I want to believe him and it would be so easy to. I can end it all it right now and go on pretending until I forget it all together.

I look at the burnt red streak on my shirt, dab at it, and hold it to my eyes. Grandpa's bloodstains on my hand. His blood on me. His blood in me. I want it to be good blood.

My eyes land on the day's mail piled on the dining room table.

An idea.

I look again at the blood on my hand.

After a moment, I say, "He was a little touched in the head. That's true."

Grandpa lets out a deep sigh and after a moment says, "I always felt kind of sorry for the guy, wondered if maybe there was some way we might have helped him that could have prevented what happened."

Broken parts, I thought.

Grandpa moves in close to me and cautiously rests a hand on my shoulder.

"Hey, what say I get us a couple more drinks?"

I glance again at the mail on the table.

"Yeah," I answer. "I think we could both probably use another one. Thanks."

When he exits the room, I grab the mail from the dining room table and pull out one of Grandma's hospital bills that had been delivered that day. I slide it into my back pocket and sit back down in my chair.

Grandpa returns and hands me my drink.

"Here you go. Made it just the way you like it—extra strong."

He takes a big drink of his Scotch, exhales an approving hiss, and holds the half-empty glass up to his.

"And mine, extra stronger."

He winks at me and I smile weakly.

"You're running with the big dogs now, Tuck. Be careful."

"I'm sorry, Grandpa," I say, but he waves it off.

"No," I continue. "I am. It's just … I started getting these anonymous letters out at the cemetery saying Slim Jim didn't kill Katie."

"That's what set you off on me? A letter from some anonymous crackpot?"

"Sounds stupid, I know. I guess I'm still not in my right mind yet."

He gives me a grandfatherly grin that lets me know I am forgiven and then he takes another swig of Scotch.

Looking over the top of the glass at me, he says, "So you been talking to Alvin Keller, huh?"

"Yep."

Then he lifts the glass again and pours the remainder of that firewater down his throat, swallowing it in three easy gulps—mouth open wide, eyes like saucers, features exaggerated by the glass in front of his face and the alcohol inside of me.

My what sharp teeth you have, I think.

My hands caress the rim of my own glass and I twirl it slowly around on the table.

"It took a while, but he eventually showed himself—it was Keller writing those letters at Slim Jim's grave. That's how I found out that he was the anonymous tipster. Told me that story of you leaving Heather alone, but I was thinking Heather was with us in Glidden. Now, that I think about it, though … I guess I'm not so sure. That was an awfully long time ago. Anyway, you can see how that got me to wondering, right?"

"Yeah, sure. I can see that, but … Christ, Tuck, I'm your Grandpa. Hows 'bout a little benefit of the doubt?"

"I know, I know. Anyway, that Old Man got me so screwed up with some of the shit he was telling me … I wasn't thinking straight. Crazy old man, small town rumors. I should know better."

Then I lead him out a little further.

I lift my face to meet his gaze, contrive a look of embarrassment and say, "The thing is ... the thing is, Grandpa ..."

"What?" he prompts, seeming more amused than anything else, but with a touch of concern behind the laughter.

"It's like I said, Grandpa, he really got to me. I mean, I believed him to the point that I actually, I don't know, dug into it a little. You know?"

"Whadya mean *dug into it*?"

"You know, I looked into it. Investigated, I guess you could say."

His eyebrows move together ever so slightly and his eyes narrow.

"Investigated, huh? Christ, that was twenty years ago, Tuck. What the hell is there to investigate?"

"More than you'd think, actually. See, they kept the evidence. All these years they kept the evidence up at the Sheriff's office."

"You don't say?"

"I do. It's been in a little shoebox in a backroom. Just sitting there collecting dust all these years."

"How 'bout that."

"Yeah, how about that," I volley back, the words coming out a little sharper than I had intended.

I affect a tender smile and sip my drink.

"So, Sheriff Buck, he let you have a look at it, did he?"

Then he lurches forward and from the edge of his seat says, "What did you find in the shoebox, Tuck—shoes?"

The whiskey is starting to hit him now. He laughs hard and leans back in his seat again.

"No, no shoes. But there was a plastic bag with some of her belongings."

"Belongings?"

"Oh, you know, things that she was wearing and carrying with her that day. Even the bag has a few hairs in it that don't like they're Katie's and there were stains on the clothes, too. I figure maybe they could be from the killer—you know, blood or spit or ..."

I get up from my chair.

"So anyway, turns out that there's a lot they can do with evidence these days that they couldn't do back then."

"Yeah? Like what?"

"Like DNA testing."

Grandpa sets his empty glass on the end table and walks toward the bay window. He wipes a hand over his mouth to clean away the froth around his lips.

"Anyway, I uh ... well, Grandpa, I ended up—let's say 'borrowing'—a hair sample from your comb—not the easiest of tasks, by the way," I say with a smile.

He starts to say something, stops.

Raises his hand, lowers it.

Wipes a hand across his mostly bald head, which is starting to glisten with sweat.

I continue.

"So, I take that hair of yours and the bag of evidence and I take them to this girl I went to school with—Laurie Monroe. You remember her, don't ya? Norma and Glenn's daughter. Real smart girl. Anyway, I take them to Laurie at the county hospital to do a DNA comparison. You know they can do that now? I mean, technically Laurie shouldn't be doing this, but you know how it is with old friends."

Best buds forever.

Suddenly, like someone has just yelled "draw," Grandpa turns to face me with his trigger finger pointed at my chest.

"Jesus Christ, Tuck! You, you, what, you hear some bullshit story from a hundred years ago and just, what, just forget everything else? Just forget everything and turn on your own family?"

"I know, I know. I'm sorry. I don't know what else I can say. I just, I haven't been myself lately—you know, with the baby and all—and then Keller hits me with this stuff and...I don't know, I guess I needed something else to think about."

Outside, a boy and a girl ride by on their bikes.

Maybe they're going to The Garden.

"Well … what can these tests prove anyhow?" he asks.

"The truth. That you're innocent and I'm an ass for ever thinking otherwise."

"Ok, good. That's good."

A puzzled look falls over him. He is processing things. Again he starts to say something and stops himself.

He turns away from me and looks out the window.

"Well … what if …"

This is it. This is where he breaks.

Or where he doesn't.

Seconds pass. Life stops. And then …

"What if they make a mistake?"

And *I know.* With that one little question I now know for sure.

I know.

And part of what I know is how wrong I was about everything I ever thought I knew before.

The clocks begin ticking again. Life has returned.

"A mistake?"

"Well, yeah, sure. What if they do something wrong and it looks like they might match or somethin'?"

"No, Grandpa, it doesn't work that way. If they match, well then …"

He turns to look at me.

"Then that would make you Katie's killer."

I inch toward him.

"So it's not going to match, right? Right, Grandpa?" I repeat louder.

Then lowering my face in front of him to catch his gaze.

"Right?"

He jerks his eyes back up, back to the moment and says, "What's that?"

"How else could your DNA match the DNA from Katie's underwear?"

"A mistake. Like I said, they could make a mistake."

"No. I told you, it doesn't work that way. They can't make a mistake like that."

"Christ, Tuck, I wish to hell you hadn't dragged me into this mess. That was a hundred years ago. It was someone else."

And now for my bluff.

From my back pocket I pull out the envelope that contains Grandma's hospital bill. I flash it in front of him long enough for him to see the hospital logo.

"As luck would have it, I got the results back from the hospital today. Didn't think Laurie would be able to run the tests so quickly, but here we are."

He stands in silence. Blood gone from his face. Air wheezing from his mouth and nose. Big circular stains have formed each armpit. His chest is heaving so hard I wonder if this is what a heart attack looks like from the outside.

"What am I going to find in here, Grandpa?"

Again the look on his face takes me back to the night Katie had gone missing when I had begged him to tell me he was going to find her. A look that a child might see as sorrow, but an adult recognizes as guilt.

I thought about the doctor from my nightmare. How he had winked at me and smiled that razor-blade smile, holding the dead child out in front of him. The same way Grandpa had done with Tory that day she'd gone missing. Had I somehow known this all along?

I begin to tear the envelope open.

"Tuck," he says, thrusting a hand out toward me.

"What, Grandpa? What is it? Is there something you want to tell me?"

I pause, think about Katie. Maybe it was a prayer.

"Pedophile," I say, spitting the word at him.

"Killer."

The words come out in a voice that I don't recognize as my own.

He gulps and lowers his hand.

"No," he says. "No. That wasn't me. That's not who I am. That was a hundred years ago."

The clocks tick through the moment. The only evidence that the world hadn't stopped again.

"Tell you what," I say. "I don't want to know what's inside. You understand me? I DON'T WANT TO KNOW!" I yell, slapping him across the face with the envelope at the same time.

I pull back, step away, catch my breath. He cowers in his chair, unwilling to look at me.

"I already know, but I don't want to know. So, here's what I'm going to do. It's nine o'clock. I'm going to put this envelope back in my pocket and I'm going to walk up to Mustang's and I'm going to drink until I can't see straight. And when the bar closes at two and it's time for my drunk ass to come back here, I'm going to open up this envelope and I'm going to read the results. Then I'm going to come back here, Grandpa. Once I know what I already know, I'm going to come back here and I'm going to ... I'm going to deal with it. You understand me? Five hours from now, I'm going to deal with things. Don't waste these five hours trying to come up with excuses or lies. Use these hours like they're your last."

Slowly, I carry my bluff to the front door, open it, and walk out without looking back.

***

He is gone when I get home from Mustang's that night. I couldn't see where he had packed anything, no real signs that he'd left for good. In fact, there were only two things that I knew for sure were missing. One was his pick-up truck and the other was that picture of him and Grandma on their wedding day. That picture of the person he always wanted to be. And had been, I suppose—a hundred and one years ago.

***

Disappearing right after his wife had died, everyone could only speculate that the grief had been too much for him.

"Poor old Hollis," friends said, "he couldn't stand the thought of being without her."

"Poor Dad." Paula said. "It hurt him so much to see mom in pain that he couldn't even visit her in the hospital."

"Poor Grandpa, he'll be back in time. When he's ready he'll come back to us."

But I knew. I knew that the place he had gone was not a place you come back from. Ever.

Poor old Hollis Gaines.

***

The day after Grandpa left, I found another grave letter at Ethan's grave. Between what was written on the lines of those pages and what I read between them, I finally found out the truth of what had happened to Katie Cooper …

***

Katie had come looking for me that afternoon, wanting to make sure I was okay after what had happened at the basketball court with Edie and Son. But Grandma had taken me, Gavin, and Heather shopping in Glidden. Grandpa was home alone watching television and drinking whiskey from his flask when Katie came to the front door looking for me.

"He went to town with his grandmother," he said, hiding the flask behind his back.

"Oh," she said. "Ok. Um, Mr. Gaines, did he seem okay?"

"Yeah, sure, far as I could tell he seemed fine. Why, what's wrong? You want to come in and wait? They won't be gone too long."

He shut the door behind her and took another swig of whiskey, then again tucked it away in his back pocket.

"Have a seat, sweetheart. I'll turn something on the television for you."

He watched her as she walked across the room to the couch, running her hands behind her as she sat to press down a skirt she wasn't wearing. His eyes burned and he swallowed the cotton out of his mouth. Licked his lips. He felt old Jack Daniels walking around inside him. Warming his belly, stirring him, inviting in those unnatural thoughts that his sober mind constantly struggled against.

He wasn't struggling now. It felt good not to struggle.

Then, falling back in the chair across from her, he said, "Well, well, you are sure turning into a fine young lady, Miss Katie."

"Thank you, Mr. Gaines."

"Yes. Yes, indeed. Miss Katie, the fine young lady. Come on, stand up and let me get a good look at you."

When she politely refused, something inside him began to rise up. The rebirth of something that had always been alive, but didn't always live—because of the struggle.

But he wasn't struggling now.

He pulled the flask out of his pocket and drank until it was gone. He tossed it to the side and said, "Okay, then. I guess I'm just going to have to come over there."

He moved next to her on the couch and cupped her face, holding her head up like an offering. Then he lifted her from the couch and made her stand in front of him.

"Yes, indeed. Miss Katie, the fine young lady."

Looking down his nose and smiling, he said, "Such a pretty little girl. Step back for a second, let me see the whole picture."

"You sure are growing up fast, aren't you, Katie?" His heart raced as he took her hands in his.

Frightened now, Katie just shrugged her shoulders.

"Oh, come on," he slurred. "You must know what a big girl you're becoming, don't you?"

"I guess," she said with a shrug. "I should probably get going, Mr. Gaines. Could you tell Tucker I was here?"

"And so pretty, too. Pretty all over."

"Pretty here," he said touching her face.

"Pretty on the outside and pretty on the inside," he said, pressing his hand against her chest and holding it there.

"In fact, you are so pretty, Katie, that I could just eat you up."

The last few words were growled out as he lurched at Katie, grabbed her by both shoulders and pulled her into him, wrapping his arms completely around her.

"I need to get going, Mr. Gaines. My mom's expecting me," she said in a meek voice that made him think of Little Red Riding Hood.

Then, cheek to cheek, he said to her, "What's the matter, Katie? Don't be afraid. Do I look like the Big Bad Wolf to you, Katie?"

Strangely, when she began to cry, it calmed him completely and he said, "Ssshh. Don't struggle, Katie. Trust me, it feels good not to struggle."

At some point in the insidiousness that followed, Katie cried a little too loud and he put his hands over her face to quiet her. He did not notice when she had stopped making any kind of noise at all.

"How did this happen?" he had wondered. This was not what he wanted. This was not who he was.

Panicked, he wrapped her lifeless body in bed sheets he had pulled from the hall closet. He went to the kitchen and pulled down a bottle of Scotch. He took a long drink and it calmed him. Grandma was going to be back from Glidden soon, so he had to act fast.

He carried Katie's body to the garage and laid it on the floor. Then he backed his truck into his garage, put Katie's lifeless body in the truck bed and threw a crumpled tarp over the top of her, weighing down the edges with bricks. He dumped the body in the high weeds along the side of the train tracks leading out of Willow Grove.

Later on, as the entire town searched the streets of Willow Grove for Katie, Grandpa pulled Keller aside and planted his lie about seeing Slim Jim and Katie. He was actually surprised at how easily he was able to persuade his old bud Alvin to make that phone call to the sheriff's office.

"It was coming back into town that I saw them, Alvin. Saw Katie and that drifter right at the railroad tracks together. Must have been about 4:30."

Affecting a tone of harried confusion, he continued, "Mary Lynn would kill me if she knew I'd left little Heather alone in the house like that—even if she was napping. And what kind of witness would that make for anyway? A grandfather who's left his baby granddaughter alone so he can go get schnockered—and then driving drunk on top of it? I'd hate to think Slim Jim would get away with this just because I screwed up, Alvin."

"So, what do we do, Hollis? What do we do if the anonymous tip isn't enough?"

At this Grandpa grabbed Alvin by the shoulders and gave him the most earnest look he could muster. "Alvin, if that time comes, I need you to tell folks that it was you who saw that hobo with that Cooper girl by the railroad tracks. It was him who killed her, Alvin. You know that. A complicated story and he may walk. Not to mention the trouble it could bring on me. I may be a drunk, Alvin, but I'm no liar. And I know what I saw. Hell, we all know it was Slim Jim killed that girl, right?"

"Right, right."

Old Man Keller paused for a long moment and with a determined and distant look he said, "Sheriff Buck, I'm calling to say that I think I know who killed that Cooper girl."

***

The grave letter contains no real apology. No accountability. Grandpa was confessing to someone else's guilt.

***

... it wasn't me, Tucker. It was that demon I told you about, the monster I hid from everyone. And I know how to make it so he can never hurt me or anyone else ever again. Your grandpa is gonna kill the demon ...

***

When I finish reading, I fold up the letter and slip it back inside the envelope. It represents the death of so much that I briefly consider digging a tiny grave and burying the letter itself. But I had buried too much in my life, so instead, I walk the graveyard with that letter safely in my hands, taking in the sight of the many-colored envelopes adorning the graves. Reading the names on each headstone as I pass, searching for one name in particular.

Buck.

Hearts Left Behind

We go to Church on Father's Day.

I sit dead center in the middle of the pew with a straight and clear path to the altar laid out in front of me. I can still see Ethan's tiny white coffin at the end of it.

Behind the altar on the east wall of the church, the stained glass image of an open-armed Jesus confronts me. He is larger than He has ever been and His eyes meet mine.

"Tucker, would you mind holding Griffin while I dig out a towel?" my cousin Allison asks.

Griffin, who had been born three weeks after Ethan, has spit up and Allison is looking for something to clean her lapel with.

"Sure."

His chest expands and air whistles from his nose. I close my eyes and hold him tight to my chest, listening to the lovely sound of his blessed breathing. Tears began to trickle down my face, leaving my mouth salty. I open my eyes to again see the arms of Jesus still opened before me and I hold that baby boy tighter, cannot imagine letting go.

When Allison sees me crying, she realizes what's going through me.

"Oh, Tucker. How stupid of me. I'm so sorry."

"It's okay. Really."

"No, it's not. That was really insensitive. I'm so sorry."

I sit back down and wait for the faithful to file out. When all have left, I look up once more at Stained-Glass Jesus and I thank Him for the gift he'd just given me. The gift of a breathing baby in my arms.

***

After church, Tammy takes Tory back to the house to finish packing up our things. We are leaving Willow Grove and with Grandma and Grandpa both gone now, I am not sure when I will return to this place again.

I take one last walk up to the playground, but Swinging Girl isn't there. Her swing isn't only empty, it's broken. The chain has snapped on one side and the seat hangs helplessly from the other. I sit down in the swing next to it and try to make sense of the past few weeks.

I suppose that I found what I was supposed to find in Willow Grove, even if it hadn't been what I was looking for. Maybe we always find what we're meant to find.

I think about the odd marvel of the Grave Letters and wonder whether the townspeople of Willow Grove will continue writing them. I hope so. It feels like something beautiful that should continue. And other than helping start those letters, I don't think I've done much *good* here. I just hope that I've done some *right*. Right by James Johnson. Right by the Coopers. Right by me and my family. Most importantly, I hope I have done right by Katie and Ethan. I want them to be proud of me.

I kick at the gravel beneath me and look again at the empty swing dangling to my left.

Just another broken part.

Maybe Old Man Keller was right. Maybe we are all just a bunch of broken parts. Broken souls walking on the grass that he mows until we became one of the broken bodies that lie beneath it.

I get up from the swing and leave the park without looking back. I was ready to leave Willow Grove. I was ready to go home.

I keep seeing you out of the corner of my eye,
But I can never seem to get you in focus.

I keep loving you in the corner of my heart
But that love just never seems to be enough.

I keep thinking of you in the corner of my mind
But I can't seem to find a memory there.

And I keep holding these arms open for you
But you won't come and warm them.

I can't live without you, son.
But I will.

Author's Note

If you enjoyed this story, a positive review on Amazon or Goodreads would be greatly appreciated. I also encourage you to visit my blog page or my facebook page.

Derek's site: http://derekrempfer.wordpress.com/
Facebook: https://www.facebook.com/derek.rempferwriter
Goodreads: https://www.goodreads.com/book/show/20603652
Amazon: http://www.amazon.com/dp/B00OTPG8VW/